of Special Imp...
to our American Readers

The Case of the
24 MISSING TITLES ...

Over the years many of our American readers have been distressed that Harlequin Romances were published in Canada three months ahead of the United States release date.

We are pleased to announce that effective April 1972 Harlequin Romances will have simultaneous publication of new titles throughout North America.

To solve the problem of the 24 MISSING TITLES (No. 1553 to No. 1576) arrangements will be made with many Harlequin Romance retailers to have these missing titles available to you before the end of 1972.

Watch for your retailer's special display!

If, however, you have difficulty obtaining any of the missing titles, please write us.

Yours truly,

The Publisher
HARLEQUIN ROMANCES.

WELCOME

TO THE WONDERFUL WORLD

of Harlequin Romances!

Interesting, informative and entertaining,
each Harlequin Romance portrays an appealing
love story. Harlequin Romances take you
to faraway places — places with real people
facing real love situations — and
you become part of their story.

As publishers of Harlequin Romances, we're extremely
proud of our books (we've been publishing
them since 1954). We're proud also that Harlequin
Romances are North America's most-read
paperback romances.

Eight new titles are released every month and are
sold at nearly all book-selling stores across
Canada and the United States.

A free catalogue listing all available Harlequin Romances
can be yours by writing to the

HARLEQUIN READER SERVICE,
M.P.O. Box 707, Niagara Falls, N.Y. 14302.
Canadian address: Stratford, Ontario, Canada.

or use order coupon at back of book.

We sincerely hope you enjoy reading
this Harlequin Romance.

Yours truly,

THE PUBLISHERS
 Harlequin Romances

PRIDE'S BANNER

by

MARJORIE NORRELL

HARLEQUIN BOOKS

TORONTO • WINNIPEG

First published in 1969 by Mills & Boon Limited,
17 - 19 Foley Street, London, England

SBN 373-01545-3

© Mills & Boon 1969

Harlequin Canadian edition published December, 1971
Harlequin U.S. edition published March, 1972

Printed in Canada

'Poor words unsaid, dreams that can never be,
Pride holds its banner between you and me.'

Anon.

CHAPTER 1

NONA HOYLE reached out a slender but strong and well-shaped hand and switched off the home hair-dryer. Without that noise she might possibly be able to hear what Avice was saying—that was, she grinned wickedly to herself, if it was anything interesting enough to want to listen to!

"And they say he's supposed to be *engaged*, if you please, to some Sister or other at Emley General. That's where he was before he was appointed here, you know."

"And have you a record as to his medical school, his pre-medical education and his home background as well?" Nona teased, but her eyes were sober enough, Avice realised, colouring.

"I know what you mean," she said sullenly, sweeping a pile of magazines into a corner and deciding she would continue to look for that knitting pattern she wanted some other time. "You think we're all a bit touched or something, don't you?" she demanded defensively. "Maybe we are, but I'd rather be touched about some man—especially one as handsome and pleasant as our new S.S.O.—than hump myself into a corner every time anything male so much as addressed a word to me in passing! You do, you know, Nona! Ever since . . ."

"Ever since Trevor Brady married Alma Vaughan without even the courtesy of breaking his supposed engagement with me, you mean, don't you?" Nona said, hoping with all her heart that her lighthearted tone and smiling face was deceiving her friend as it had deceived them all for so long now. She was almost beginning to believe herself that she had not really cared for Trevor and that it hadn't really hurt when he went home on vacation and married the girl he'd known all his life, writing her when the actual ceremony was over!

"Something like that," Avice muttered shame-facedly, then she straightened up and turned to look directly into Nona's blue eyes, her own slanting green ones shining with her repressed indignation.

"It's true, anyway!" she asserted. "Before that you were like the rest of us, ready for a bit of fun, a flirtation, something to take care of those black hours we all get, when we can't see any future except going on and on until we become replicas of Sister Jarvis! I think I'd rather have *any* fate than that!"

"There's no reason to grow like Sister Jarvis, so far as I can see," Nona returned, smiling. It never took more than a moment for her to recover her customary friendly, happy nature even when, as now, someone had reminded her of other less happy days. "What about Sister Maxwell? I'm sure nobody would mind growing up to be like *her*! I know I wouldn't!"

"Or Matron!" Avice returned, and then, for no real reason except that the new Matron, Miss Frost, was such a change from the one who had retired a year ago, the thought of the contrast between the two made them both go off into a series of giggles.

"Depends which Matron!" Nona remarked, and when Avice, naturally, said 'Miss Frost, of course,' it seemed the momentary little upset had quite disappeared.

Unfortunately it seldom seemed possible for Avice to allow any subject to drop once she had started to discuss it, and within seconds, exactly as she had expected, Nona was forced to listen to a new list of the wonderful attributes the nursing staff were attaching to the new S.S.O., Mr. Roper.

Craig Roper! She thought of his name as she closed her ears to Avice's chatter about what he had said that morning as he left the theatre. Herself theatre staff nurse, Nona was quite content to meet Craig Roper in the

8

theatre, look after him to the best of her ability, stand in awe of his truly wonderful surgery . . . and to keep clear, except when duty made it imperative for them to speak to one another.

"Well," she remarked, cutting short Avice's words simply because she was tired of listening to the same remarks she had heard most of the staff of St. Jude's make almost every day since his arrival there, "all I can say is he's very good in Theatre. He's considerate, which is more than Mr. Rawlingson was! He's an excellent surgeon, tidy and quick in his movements, and he doesn't make any more work for the nurses than is absolutely unavoidable! The best thing about him is that he's always pleasant. Maybe if he's about to be married in the near future that's the reason. He's happy . . . and happy people are usually easy to get along with, or so I've found."

"Anyway," the unrepentant Avice was brushing her fiery-red hair with quick, firm strokes, "he's not married *yet*! Benson says her sister's at Emley, and she knows the Sister he's engaged to. She says she's an iceberg, pure and not so simple! Can't imagine any man, especially a man like Craig Roper, being content to remain either engaged or married to an iceberg! He doesn't look that sort. While there's life there's hope, they say. Until he's *married* to his Sister Drayton, I say he's fair game!"

"Well, count me out of all your little schemes and ideas, will you?" Nona yawned. "I'm off to bed. I did intend to give myself a face pack tonight. We said we'd have a beauty session, and all I've done is wash my hair! You haven't even done *that*!"

"I'll have it done in two jiffs," Avice promised, "but I'm going down to the supermarket first! Wouldn't you like one of those package curries for your supper?"

"No, thanks all the same!" Nona shuddered. "I don't know how you can face things like that and contemplate

9

duty in the morning! I can't! I haven't got that sort of good-natured stomach!"

"Well," Avice countered, laughing, "I know I haven't what's vulgarly known as your kind of 'guts'! *I* should have gone under, if what happened to you eighteen months ago had happened to me! I do admire you, you know, Nona." She was suddenly serious. "I'm really sorry if my teasing annoyed you!"

"That's all right," Nona said lightly. "Forget it. And you don't know how you'd have reacted to something which has, so far, never happened to you! There's such a thing as pride, you know. It may well be called one of the seven deadly sins, but there are times when it undoubtedly has its uses, you know! If you don't hurry up," she warned, "the supermarket will be closed! I know this late-opening idea's catching on, but I don't think customers who come at the very last minute, especially when they're having late-night opening hours anyway to help folks who can't shop at normal hours, will be really welcome. I'll put the kettle on. You can dry your hair while we eat supper."

With Avice gone from the flat the two shared since they had unitedly achieved staff nurses' status and received permission to live out from the Nurses' Home, Nona did not immediately begin to busy herself on the setting of the table, the filling of the kettle and the other few chores they shared on these evenings when they were both at home on the same evening.

Avice's words about her own reactions to the male sex had been a trifle disconcerting, yet what was she to do? Nona asked herself the question for at least the hundredth time since she had received that brief, hurtful note from Trevor telling of his marriage to Alma Vaughan, a girl who had left St. Jude's the previous year, a girl he had known all his life and with whom he had met up again while on holiday in the Lake District.

She was over it now, she assured herself firmly, but

nothing would ever erase the memory of that awful morning when she had recognised his handwriting on the envelope and opened it, never dreaming what message the letter inside contained.

She had made up her mind as to the right lines her conduct must take the moment she had re-read the letter for the third time and made absolutely certain there was no mistake and that the words she had thought she had read really were written there and, it seemed, in her heart and brain for ever.

She had folded the brief letter very carefully, almost meticulously, then she had turned to Avice who sat beside her at breakfast that day.

"I'm no longer engaged," she had said quietly. "Trevor's married someone else. He hasn't asked for the ring back . . . says he'd like me to keep it in memory of him. Would you like it . . . as a birthday gift or something?" then she hurried from the dining-room and left it to Avice to spread the news on the hospital grapevine, knowing all the girls in her year would be sympathetic, but wouldn't confront her with the knowledge of how big a fool she had been made to look in the eyes of everyone in the hospital.

She had managed to keep up a brave front all the time, although none of them guessed—at least she *hoped* none of them guessed—at the tears she shed in the night when she was supposed to be sleeping, or of the long, solitary walks she had undertaken whenever she was off duty, simply to avoid coming into contact with anyone who might have guessed the extent of her hurt and have been tempted to offer sympathy. Sympathy, she had felt then, was the last thing she wanted.

Miss Barrowclough, almost due to retire, might have been, as Avice always referred to her, 'an old dragon' where most of her nurses were concerned, but to the girl she summoned to her presence as soon as the news of

Nona's private grief reached her ears, she had been wisdom and kindness themselves.

"You may have leave, if you wish it, Nurse," she said in a kindly tone, her steel-grey eyes looking straight into Nona's blue ones, "but I don't advise it. My advice may seem hard to accept, but I do assure you it works. Your work is excellent as it is; could you not absorb yourself even a little further? As theatre staff nurse, for example? I think you would find it very rewarding . . . and an excellent aid to the dismissal of anything which may be troubling you at the moment."

She had made no direct reference to the broken engagement, but Nona realised she knew all about it and that she was trying to help in what seemed the best way. At the time Nona hadn't felt she could agree, but now, with the passing of time, she realised how right Matron had been.

If she had accepted the leave and gone home, Aunt Mary would have fussed, Uncle Jack would have raved and stormed about Trevor, and she knew she would have felt irritated with them both, darlings though they were. No, the better solution had been the one Miss Barrow-clough had suggested, and when she had also suggested Nona might like to find a friend willing to share a flat with her and to live out, that too had been a help.

In their early days as flat-mates Avice had been carefully guarded in all she said about the love-affairs of their friends, the past excitement of the romance between Nurse Hoyle and the R.S.O. as Trevor had been in those days. It was only lately, she reflected, making herself get up from the low easy chair where she had been sitting to dry her hair, that Avice had mentioned Nona's attitude to men, an attitude she had forced herself to adopt since the morning Trevor's letter had arrived.

"Never become involved . . . not ever again," she had faced her reflection in her small mirror in the shared bedroom at the Nurses' Home. "I *must* remember that!

I don't need a man! Matron isn't married, and she seems happy enough. I can have my work, and my friends, and that's going to be enough for me. I won't ever lay myself wide open to going through all this, not ever again! There isn't a man who's worth it!"

She had kept to her resolve and found, that in the beginning it wasn't too hard to avoid being a member of mixed company, because she was still too hurt. The fact that she *was* hurt enabled her to refuse invitations quietly and without fuss, and by the time the hurt had worn off a little most of the men with whom she came into contact each day felt they knew what her answer would be if they invited her out, and just didn't!

She had fun, of course. If there happened to be a party and she was invited, she went along, but always alone or in a group, never in a twosome or foursome. When a new male member of staff came along, as Craig Roper had come six short months ago, she didn't join in any of the discussions about him, paid no attention to the gossip of the grapevine, but kept herself aloof, being polite and faintly friendly, but never anything more.

"It's much the best way," she reaffirmed to herself as she put the finishing touches to the supper-table. "I couldn't care less what sort of woman he's engaged to, or whether or not it's true he's bought that big house in Oakfield Avenue! That's his business, and I hope everything works out all right for him, that's all."

When Avice returned it appeared she had seen the pathologist out in his car and the woman by his side had been Miss Redfern, the new assistant gynae at St. Jude's. The subject of their probable friendship and whether or not Miss Redfern had "gone off" Mr. Semple kept Avice occupied for the remainder of the evening. It was only long after the lights were out and even the sound of Avice's transistor was stilled that Nona returned to her thoughts of the day when, or so it had seemed at the time, all her hopes and dreams had been shattered.

"But they hadn't," she told herself firmly, turning her cheek into the pillow and settling down to sleep. "Work's much more rewarding than depending on someone else's whims! At least one knows where one is when there's no one else to please except the doctors, Matron *and* where it's possible, the patient!" and on this reflection she closed her eyes and within minutes was sleeping soundly.

The slight disquiet that Avice's words had aroused with their wakening of memories she had believed buried for ever had disappeared by morning. She woke before Avice—not an unusual occurrence—and made breakfast before she called her friend. Avice was on Women's Medical, and both of them on duty at eight in the morning. It was always a rush to get the number four bus on the corner, especially as the newly opened plastics factory just outside the town had so many workers living in and around the block of flats, but most of the conductors and conductresses knews the nurses well and usually managed to squeeze them on, even if the bus appeared full.

They parted outside the cloakroom where they left a set of clean cuffs, a clean apron and change of shoes. It was Avice's turn to make the evening meals this week, and as they parted she called in a conspiratorial whisper: "Goulash . . . O.K.?" and, smiling, Nona nodded.

She made her way to the theatre smiling happily. Nona loved cooking, but she liked the less intricate dishes on which Aunt Mary had brought her up and the cooking of which to perfection she had handed on to her niece.

Avice, on the other hand, had never before had the opportunity to cook anything more complicated than a boiled egg, and she delighted in purchasing all the current books on the cooking of out-of-the-ordinary dishes she could find . . . and insisted upon trying them out on herself and her flat-mate. Sometimes, viewing Avice's procession of boy-friends, Nona caught herself wondering just what kind of man he would have to be to put up with this endless attempt to "tickle his palate," as Avice termed her search of the unusual, and then, reminding herself that all sorts of people ate all sorts of dishes since they had taken to so much travelling abroad, she dismissed the matter from her mind and went into Theatre to make certain everything was in readiness for the work of the day.

There was, as always, a full list. Two complicated femurs, one hernia, two appendectomies, one peptic ulcer, a colostomy and three or four haemorrhoids, bunions and other similar operations to be done.

Everything went as smoothly as it had always done since Craig Roper had come to St. Jude's. Matt Paling, the anaesthetist, beamed as he set up his machine. In the days before Craig arrived, and when Mr. Rawlingson had been S.S.O. before going on to a more important post somewhere in the Midlands, Matt Paling's face had often been pale and drawn even before the morning session in the theatre had started. Thomas R. J. Rawlingson, to give him his full title, had been what was commonly known throughout the hospital as "a bind." Nothing ever was right for him. He found fault with everything and everyone, and most of the nurses were terrified of his loud voice, his sarcastic tongue.

Now all that was a thing of the past. Little Nurse Stephenson hurried about taking instruments from the steriliser, looking as busy and as important as she was made to feel.

Sister's expression as she watched Nona completing her tasks, checked on the work already done, was one of supreme content. Nona, although as quiet and as controlled as always, felt a satisfaction in her work which had never been present in the Theatre until Craig Roper had arrived at St. Jude's. Altogether, her thoughts ran as they waited for Craig to appear, life in Theatre at St. Jude's was better now than it had ever been for as long as anyone could remember.

Exactly on the stroke of the hour Craig came striding along the white-tiled corridor. That was another wonderful and pleasant thing about him, he was always on time! Mr. Rawlingson was invariably late, and equally invariably was prone to blame the fact upon anyone who had experienced the misfortune to have come into contact with him earlier in the day, ranging from his housekeeper who, according to him, had been late serving breakfast, to Williamson, his chauffeur, who, he said, hadn't the sense to know the High Street was always crowded on Thursday mornings.

Craig, as yet, had no chauffeur and drove himself in his dignified saloon. But Craig, she reflected, wasn't also a consultant as yet! Raymond Julian Rawlingson had been Consultant at The Home, a private nursing home outside the town, of which, she had heard rumours, he had been part-founder when his grandfather had left him a considerable capital sum in shares.

Craig, so the grapevine had it, had no housekeeper either, but lived alone, save for the attentions of a thrice-weekly help, Mrs. Lom, who was also a cleaner at St. Jude's and from whom the grapevine gleaned a great deal of information.

It had been Mrs. Lom, for instance, who had informed everyone that having an already established rose garden had been one of the main deciding factors in Craig's purchase of Grey Walls, the large house which stood alone, almost in the centre of Oakfield Avenue, the most select avenue in Whemlybridge.

"Sez 'is intended 'as a fondness for roses!" Mrs. Lom's expressive sniff had concluded the remark, but whether to signify she too loved the scent of roses in bloom or whether to express her disgust at such a "fancy-some" attitude—that being one of her favourite expressions—it was hard to say.

Whether the story was a true one or not, Nona had heard from one of the nurses that, every morning since he had started work in Whemlybridge on the first of July, Craig Roper had appeared at the hospital with a rose or a rosebud in his buttonhole.

With his arrival in Theatre everything became simply a part of routine. One by one the cases were despatched, some of them operations lasting more than an hour, others no longer than twenty minutes or so, but all of them obviously equal in importance where Craig Roper was concerned.

That, Nona decided as he scrubbed up after the last operation and prepared to divest himself of his gown— the third that morning—was one of the nicest things about him. All patients, where he was concerned, seemed to be of the utmost importance the moment they came under his personal care. With Raymond Julian there had been an entirely different attitude, and sometimes she had wondered just how he behaved when he was working at The Home.

"Very differently, you bet your sweet life!" had been Avice's comment when Nona had expressed this thought to her one evening. "He's got an eye on the main chance —always had, even before he had that money left to him—now he's determined to get to the top of his own particular tree, and I wouldn't mind betting he doesn't much care whose neck he steps on as a rung!"

Nona had protested, only half-heartedly because she wasn't really interested, but she deplored Avice's continual suspicion that everyone was, one way or the other, out to take care of number one, "And who can blame them?" she had asked, wide-eyed. Avice firmly believed, and said so repeatedly, that if one didn't look out for oneself then no one else would do so, and she certainly lived by that theory!

Nona was thinking of her friend as she checked up after Nurse Stephenson. Everything appeared to be in order, clean and sterile, ready for the next time of usage. She was walking past one of the two sinks when she caught the gleam of something and turned to check as to what it might be. There could be no mistake. It was Craig's watch, an expensive, beautiful affair with his name engraved on the back. He must have forgotten to put it on again after he had washed.

She called to Nurse Stephenson and then remembered she had told the girl to go, as she had a lecture due to start any minute now. There was nothing else for it. She would have to try and catch him and hand the watch back to him herself.

Nona, already divested of her theatre gown, hurried swiftly along the corridor and towards the doctors' sitting-room, hoping she would find him there, but despite her haste she was just in time to see his broad-shouldered form disappearing through the doors at the end of the corridor and to watch him striding away towards the staff car park.

Rules forbade her to run, but she hurried as fast as she could and, almost breathless, she managed to hail him as he slammed his car door shut and switched on the engine. With a pleasant smile he wound down his window as she attracted his attention.

"You wanted me, Staff?" he queried. "Something wrong?"

"You . . . left your watch, sir." Nona held out the watch and saw his eyes light up as he accepted it.

"Thanks," he said quietly. "It's a rather personal gift. I'd hate anything to happen to it," and with no further ado he saluted her, obviously not remembering her name and aware of her status only by her cap which denoted her as staff nurse, then he turned his full attention to the control of his vehicle, apparently ignoring her altogether.

What had she expected? She asked the question of Avice much later when they had concluded their evening meal and were trying to decide whether to go to the cinema, watch their rental television or simply to go to bed early and catch up on sleep.

"I don't know what *you* expected," the sharp note Nona did not greatly care for was back in Avice's voice, "but I do know I'd have made more use of such an opportunity than you've apparently made! I . . ." she wrinkled her brow in thought, "I'd have either kept the watch until about this time," she glanced at her watch, "and taken it round to his house! I bet I wouldn't have been kept at the door, either! If I hadn't done that, then I'd have waited until morning and met him when he arrived at St. Jude's. It would have been a grand excuse to talk—he'd have had time to have missed it by then! I don't know *what* I'd have done," she concluded crossly, "but I do know I'd have got more satisfaction than just handing the thing back with a bare word of thanks. That's all you seem to have achieved!"

"That was enough," Nona began, prepared to dismiss the matter at once, but not so Avice.

"Things like that always happen to you," she grumbled, "and you wouldn't make any capital out of it, would you? Why couldn't something like that happen to me?"

"Perhaps because you're Staff Women's Medical and not Staff Theatre," Nona teased, adding as she glanced in the cupboard, "and if either of us hopes for a morning cuppa I'd better get down to the supermarket right away! We appear to have run out of both sugar *and* tea, and with the best will in the world I never can reconcile myself to facing duty without my morning cuppa!"

CHAPTER 2

IT was an extremely lucky thing, Nona reflected as she pulled on her hooded anorak and fastened it under her chin as a protection against the thin September drizzle which had sprung up during the evening, that she knew Avice almost as well as she knew herself!

Avice was a grand girl, an excellent flat-mate, but Nona always had to keep her tongue in check whenever it was Avice's turn to shop or organise the running of the small household.

Sugar and tea were not the only things needed before morning, and by the time she left the flat she had a long list of necessities in her pocket and a capacious shopping basket hooked over her arm in readiness for the heavy load she expected to collect from the store.

She didn't mind, she enjoyed shopping, especially domestic shopping, but it was always regrettable there was so little free time to indulge her fancy for going from shop to shop, comparing price and quality as Aunt Mary had taught her to do. Supermarkets were wonderful, she thought, entering and being met by the blast of canned music which she always insisted was laid on so that people shopped without really thinking about the sum they expected to spend, but for her personal choice she much preferred the little shop on the corner which back home in Presbyton had been Aunt Mary's standby.

She walked from counter to counter, methodically ticking off the goods as she bought them from the list in her pocket. Tea, sugar, cheese, butter, biscuits, marmalade, rye bread—the special non-fattening kind Avice insisted she must have if she didn't want to lose her slender figure! Nona chuckled to herself as she pushed the package into the wire basket she was carrying. She didn't think Avice had any need to worry about putting on weight, but she always did! Nona ate more or less as she pleased and never had gone on a diet in her life. It seemed to her that, rightly or wrongly, the protein-packed foods Aunt Mary had insisted were so good for her, added to a small intake of starchy foods, little sugar and plenty of fruit, vegetables and exercise, were all that were needed to keep anyone of even fairly sound health moderately slender and healthy as well.

She was standing at the cereal counter when someone touched her arm. Nona turned, her ready smile on her lips, recognising at once the anxious face of Mrs. Belmont, whose small son had been admitted to St. Jude's a week or so earlier. Tony had chased a ball into the roadway, forgetting all his painstakingly learned lessons of kerbside drill. It was more, as Craig had remarked at the time, that his guardian angel, or his lucky star, depending on one's outlook, had been taking care of him at the time than anything else that his injuries had been as slight as they had resolved themselves into being. All the same, Mrs. Belmont had haunted the hospital for days.

"He really is getting better, isn't he, Nurse Hoyle?" she asked now. "I know that pretty Nurse Marsden on the Children's Block tells me I've no reason to worry and that Tony'll soon be home, but when I think of him, lying there in his bed, his leg and his chest all strapped up like they are . . ."

"He's very lucky to be there at all, Mrs. Belmont," Nona said firmly. "He might so easily have been killed, you know! Don't worry quite so much, if you can help it," she advised, knowing perfectly well that Nancy Marsden had said the same thing time and time again, and always without any real effect. Nona had what she always thought of as one of her inspirational flashes.

"Have you seen little Peter Jackson in the end bed?" she asked, and as Mrs. Belmont shook her head Nona hastened to continue her theory that if people like Alice Belmont could only *see* for themselves that their loved ones were not always the most seriously ill patients in the hospital, they might understand a little more just why there had to be only certain times allowed for visiting, certain times when the nursing staff must be allowed to continue their primary work—the care of all those for whose nursing they were responsible—and not feel so resentful, as Mrs. Belmont most certainly did, when the bell rang for the second time, telling them they must go.

"If you could spare a moment, the next time you visit Tony," she suggested tactfully, "perhaps you'd have a word with him? His only relatives live at Felbrough, that's a full thirty miles away, and the train service isn't too good, the bus service almost non-existent. Peter was badly burned while on holiday. He'd gone camping with some friends and there was an accident with an oil cooker or something. He's very brave, and he's had numbers of skin grafts and other such treatments, and a burn is a most painful thing from which to recover at any time. His parents can only get over once each week, and his aunt and uncle, and the cousins with whom he'd gone camping, have to leave before the bell goes— making *their* visiting time even shorter than the usual ones. If you *could* look in on him—tell him about Tony, perhaps, they're about the same age. When whichever is the first of them to get around the ward a little he'll have a ready-made friend, and you'd be doing that child a really good turn, Mrs. Belmont."

"Poor little soul!" She had, Nona was satisfied, guessed rightly in supposing Mrs. Belmont to be a sympathetic women whose heart would respond to the plight of the rather lonely little boy in the single cubicle at the end of the ward. "Can he read or anything, Nurse? I don't mean *can* he read," she hastened to explain. "I mean . . . could he hold a book, a jigsaw, or anything like that?"

"A book would be an excellent idea, I think," Nona said warmly. "He can have a portable reading desk across his bed and one of the nurses would turn the pages whenever he required that service! But it isn't so much the book," she stressed, "as the thought of someone else, besides the nurses, that is, taking an interest in how he's getting on . . . just like Tony," she emphasised.

"I'll look in on him tomorrow, Nurse," Mrs. Belmont promised. "My sister's coming over, so I can leave Tony a few minutes before it's time to go and let him have a chat with his auntie by way of a change from just his dad or me! I expect he'll be convalescent sooner or later, and have to report in at Outpatients as Tony will?" she added.

"I suppose so," Nona nodded, half expecting the words which followed.

"Well," Mrs. Belmont conceded with the air of one conferring an enormous favour, "if he's as nice a little laddie as you say, *and* if he and Tony get along all right together, make friends and all that, I don't see why he couldn't stay with us until he's finished with his visits to St. Jude's. Depends on how they get along together and if Tony likes the idea, of course.'"

"Of course," Nona said gently, knowing much better than Mrs. Belmont how quickly friendships born of a shared experience of pain, shock and fright flourish once the first horror has gone. "I don't think you'll have any real need to worry about that," she said with such conviction that Mrs. Belmont's anxious face relaxed and she smiled too. "I'll ask Nurse Marsden to look out for you tomorrow!" she promised, knowing full well there would be no need for that! Mrs. Belmont's first action after making certain her son was indeed "progressing" if only a little, was to check with the nurses that this was so!

With a final word or two about how difficult it was to keep an eye on the children all the time, look after her home and husband and answer the telephone to take the orders for the plants, shrubs, floral tributes and so on which were the source of the family income, they parted happily enough. Only when she had gone all round the store and was on her way to the exit did Nona remember that she had not, after all, collected her cereal and had to go all the way round again, since it was a one-way traffic system to help speed the shoppers!

As always happened when she did the tour twice, she found herself buying much more than she had come prepared to purchase. None of it was what Aunt Mary would have called wasteful shopping, but it all took time —and money—and her face was a little rueful as she watched the cashier totting up her purchases at the end of her second trip round the shop.

"I wonder who does Craig Roper's shopping for him?" she speculated as she watched the man who had preceded her in the queue methodically packing his purchases into a large box. "I don't suppose he'll bother about much, living alone. I expect he eats out mainly. He'll be almost bound to do that until he's married and sets up house properly."

"Thirty-seven and eightpence, please!" the voice of the cashier brought her back to earth with a bump. She counted out the money, transferred her goods from the wire basket belonging to the shop to her own, and dismissed all thoughts of Craig Roper from her mind. She might have gone on speculating about him, but someone else stopped her as she was about to leave the store. For a moment she did not recognise the young man's face, but as soon as he spoke she remembered exactly who he was and why she ought to have remembered him at first glance.

"It's Mike Robinson, isn't it?" she said, and he nodded. "Did the wedding go off all right?"

"Fine, thanks, Staff." Mike's honest face beamed in embarrassment. "We've been lucky about a small *and* inexpensive flat as well. I think it's mainly because you gave me such an excellent character reference! Patsy says that must have been what did the trick, anyhow," he concluded,

"I don't think I've as much influence as all *that*!" Nona laughed, and went on to ask more details about the flat, the wedding and so on. She wasn't pretending to be interested. Nona *was* interested in everything and everyone, particularly if they had anything at all to do with St. Jude's. It did not matter at the moment that she and Avice had not decided as yet what to do with their evening!

Mike was a porter at Judes, and Patsy had been a ward-maid there for two years. They were a pleasant, happy couple who had been married during the Bank Holiday, and only being on duty had prevented Nona from being present at the wedding. They had all been busy because of the holiday rota for all the staff ever since, and this was the first time Nona had seen either of them since the day he had shyly presented her with the handwritten invitation from Patsy's parents.

They chatted for a few minutes longer about this and that, the wedding, the brief holiday he and Patsy had taken on the coast, but, inevitably since everyone at St. Jude's seemed to want to talk about the new S.S.O., it was Mike who mentioned Craig Roper and what a pleasant person he appeared to be.

"He's wonderful to work with in Theatre," Nona said truthfully. "It's a pleasure to work with him."

"Bit different from Mr. Rawlingson, I can see that for myself!" Mike said, grinning. "He seems to be managing all right on his own in that big house as well. Patsy's brother—the one who's an interior decorator, you know —says he's busy thinking up all sorts of schemes and plans for the house. He wants his ideas drawing out on paper so's he can post 'em to his fiancée. I wonder if she knows just what a lucky girl she is, and if she really deserves him?"

"I suppose so." Nona did not care to discuss the man with whom she worked all day, every day. There appeared to be something disloyal in the action, even though she knew perfectly well neither she nor Mike would ever in any way be disloyal to anyone from Jude's. "I understand they've known one another a long time, so they ought to know pretty well just what each other thinks about almost everything . . . at least so far as decorating their mutual home's concerned."

"I'd have thought he'd have married before this," Mike went on conversationally, "once he'd got over his first years as a Registrar."

"Perhaps there were reasons why they didn't . . . marry, I mean," Nona said, and instantly found herself wondering just what sort of reasons any girl could possibly have for keeping a man like Craig Roper waiting for her answer!

There wasn't really any mystery about it, had she but known. Craig had worked out a scheme of living for himself, way back in his first year at Medical School. It was true he did not meet Ellen Drayton until almost three years after that, but his mind had been firmly made up the day he had started out on his medical career.

Success first, no matter who he met or how he felt about them! Ellen had shared his ideas when they had first started to go around together. Like Craig she dreamed of the day when he would become a Senior Surgical Officer and, later . . . not too much later, or so he had planned and dreamed, a consultant surgeon with his foot on the first rung of the ladder he fully intended to climb to the top!

His appointment as S.S.O. to St. Jude's at Whemly-bridge had seemed to him the first step towards his desired goal. It had been slightly disappointing that Ellen had not appeared to share his enthusiasm, but he had put that down to the fact that she was tired and in need of a holiday. If she'd had her way, he reflected, carefully choosing the small button mushrooms he intended to make into an omelette for himself (the eggs were already reposing on the shelf of the large old-fashioned larder attached to Grey Walls, and almost as cool as if they had been placed in the fridge which he had bought as soon as he had acquired the house) they'd have shared a poky flat somewhere, for *years*!

Ellen would be agreeably surprised, he told himself, how capable he had become, domestically speaking. He hadn't intended to do any more than heat up the occasional tin or package of soup at supper time, boil an egg or two as breakfast, and to have luncheon and dinner out, but that was proving both expensive and difficult.

He did not care for any of the three main restaurants in Whemlybridge, and having been kept waiting a very long time on the one occasion he had visited the small café known as Ann's Parlour, he had decided it would be as well if he taught himself to cook a few simple meals until Ellen joined him and could take over the domestic side of affairs.

He had been greatly surprised to discover he actually *liked* cooking, and took a real delight in trying out dishes specially recommended to him by one or other of his friends.

"Clear soup, mushroom omelette, fresh fruit and some continental coffee," he muttered to himself, reviewing his menu mentally. "That ought to see me through to-night! I'll do scrambled eggs in the morning. Mrs. Lom appears to have bought enough eggs to feed a regiment, but I like them!"

He was humming a little tune to himself as he turned in at the short, wide driveway to Grey Walls. By the time he had turned his key and opened the door the soft and gentle humming had changed to a gay lighthearted whistle which in the empty, silent house he made no attempt to suppress.

It was pleasant to enter the wide hall and be met by

the warmth of the automatic gas central heating Bob Anderson had advised him as being the best and most economical form of heating his rather large house. It had been a wise choice, he decided, turning the thermostat up a little. Ellen would be pleased. She disliked, almost above everything else, to be cold, and she was, he smiled, remembering, such a chilly creature.

There were circulars and letters piled up neatly on the small telephone table in the hall. Mrs. Lom liked to have everything orderly, even, as she somewhat cryptically remarked, there wasn't much there to keep in order . . . as yet!

The top letter on the pile was the one which had changed his low, contented humming to the gay whistle which echoed and re-echoed through the empty house. The handwriting was unmistakable, as was the postmark, and he reflected happily that evidently Ellen had not wasted much time in studying the drawings he had posted off to her only two nights ago.

It wouldn't be long now, he told himself, still whistling as, his enthusiasm suddenly upsurging, he bounded upstairs to look over the rooms which were now as familiar as those he had shared with a colleague for three long years.

The landing was wide. He pictured it in thick, dark red carpeting, the woodwork in gleaming ivory, a few well-chosen pictures framed and at varying heights on the walls. The walls themselves should, in his opinion, be papered in some very light paper, either white with embossing, or the silver-grey he had noticed in Marshall's shop last week. Of course the final choice would have to be Ellen's, since presumably she would spend much more time in the house than he, but he could picture so well the drawings he had sent to her outlining his own ideas of how the house *should* look when completely decorated and furnished. Now she had sent her answer. He would know in a few minutes whether or not their ideas still marched along the same lines as they used to do . . . how long ago was it now?

Trying to remember, it seemed a very long time since they had first talked of their "dream house." Well, he told himself, looking round the large front bedroom with its own adjacent bathroom suite, he had come a long way towards the sort of thing their dreams had fashioned.

"A solid house," Ellen had said. "The sort of house where we can put down roots! The sort of house a family would like to grow up in . . . and a garden!"

The latter requirement had not been particularly easy to fulfil in Whemlybridge. Much of the surrounding district, where, not so many years ago he might have been able to buy space for a really extensive garden, had been built up in the years of industrial expansion. He considered he had been lucky in buying Grey Walls, and doubly lucky in having acquired the established rose garden which Ellen had said so often was a life-long ambition of hers.

"There'll have to be someone to give a hand in the garden now and again," he decided. "I don't know anything about gardening, and Ellen's been a town girl so long she must have forgotten all she ever learned from her grandfather she's always quoting! We could have a greenhouse along the west wall. We could have a patio . . . do barbecues and things on summer evenings . . ."

He ran back downstairs, still happily envisaging the house when Ellen had been given time to add the feminine touches which would make so much difference even to his own ideas and scheme. Looking round him now he laughed aloud. What would she think of this "set for one" arrangement of his in the kitchen, where he had decided to take his meals while still living alone? The "set for one" had been a good idea, he decided. He had laid out a set of crockery and cutlery for all occasions, yet only for one person. Methodically, each time he had eaten, he washed up and replaced the utensils in exactly the same place.

"Time and motion expert, that's what you are, Craig my son!" he congratulated himself. "And that applies to upstairs as well!"

It did indeed. He had purchased a small camp-bed and fixed it up in the small boxroom at the end of the first floor corridor, not too far from the bathroom. It was a simple matter to make his bed, to leave it to air in the morning, and to clear away everything—shaving kit, talcum powder, toothpaste—before Mrs. Lom arrived in the morning. It was an equally simple matter to have his bed ready for use at night. He grinned to himself as he reflected how simple, how easy life was when one lived alone . . . but hot on the heels of that thought came the one which reminded him how lonely it was as well!

"I'm getting morbid!" he decided. "Ellen's probably decided when she wants the wedding . . ." and recalling that the last paragraph in his letter had asked her actually to name the day, he decided against preparing and eating his meal just now as was his habit. He'd read his letter first, make plans when he learned what she had to say.

He sat down awkwardly in the one occasional chair he had bought for himself. It was comfortable enough—he wriggled in its embrace as though to prove that fact to himself—but not the sort of chair a man would want to sit in and relax after a hard day in the theatre! Still, he decided, he wouldn't be using it much longer, although he would always have genuine affection for everything he had used in his "camping out" days at Grey Walls!

"They can go into the patio, when we've built it," he decided, then ripped the flap of the envelope and took out the single sheet of paper it contained.

For a moment he could not believe what he read, and instantly, typical of Craig, read the brief note again more slowly. There was no mistake. Ellen wasn't coming to Grey Walls at all, not even to look at it. All joy gone as though wiped away by some gigantic invisible sponge, he sat down, huddled in the chair, and took out the letter again to re-read it for the third time in just as many minutes.

CHAPTER 3

IT was true. No matter how many times he read the words over they said the same thing. Ellen was "tired of waiting." She had never expected it to be such a long time before they were established in a home of their own. She was no longer interested in the glamour of being a consultant's wife. She would, she had written, much rather be the ordinary loving wife of an ordinary equally loving G.P. who loved her enough not to mind a few risks or being poor for a time!

Craig read the letter again. It seemed so unlike the Ellen he knew, the Ellen who had, or so he believed, thought it well worth while, their four—or was it now five?—he couldn't remember exactly—long years of courtship.

He hadn't wanted her to "make do" as he had seen so many wives of his colleagues have to "make do." He wanted to start where almost everyone else thought of calling it a day and going on to do the same dreary round every day for the rest of their lives! That wasn't for him, and he hadn't wanted it for Ellen either. He had firmly believed she thought along the same lines as he did himself, that they were one in their way of looking at things like this as they intended to be in all else.

He sat back in the chair as far as possible, concentrating. He was trying to remember the long talks they had enjoyed . . . long ago now, in the beginning of their relationship. The plans they had made, so far as he was concerned, still existed. Ellen had risen from nurse to staff nurse, from staff to ward Sister, and he had believed she was as thrilled as he had been by their mutual progress. All this had been only part of their mutual plans

32

and schemes. Now, in a few lines, she had shattered the dream for ever.

Was it for ever? He looked hopefully back to the letter, telling himself she must have been suffering from one of the migraine headaches which plagued her from time to time and that she must have written this letter while still depressed.

He looked eagerly at the written page, half-expecting to find some indication that she had not been feeling well, and, when he had found it, he was quite prepared to telephone immediately and ask if she were better.

There was nothing to give any such relief to his shocked mind, instead he found a sentence which, somehow in the confusion of disbelief appeared to have previously escaped him but certainly seemed to indicate that Ellen had known exactly what she was writing when she put pen to paper; "I am to be married next month to Dr. Dearby who has a small share in the combined practice I've told you about here . . ."

There was something else over the page, and for a moment Craig hesitated, wondering what other shocks could be in store for him. Whatever they might be, he decided reluctantly, it would be as well to face them now, and slowly he turned over the page.

"We shall have a flat over the general surgery," she had written. "Until we find our feet I shall work as surgery nurse, but not for long. Neither David or myself want to leave it too late to start a family. . . ."

There was more, but Craig could not steel himself to read further. He looked round the large modern kitchen. The previous owner's wife had been a fervent admirer of American ways in the kitchen and had obviously decided that this was one room in the house which should be as modern as tomorrow. There were electricity points everywhere. There were gas points too, for additional heating appliances to augment the central heating. There were special strip lights, cunningly placed in the most strategic places where extra lighting might well be an advantage.

Craig shuddered silently as he recalled the time he had spent staring at various kitchen appliances in the showrooms of the gas and electricity boards, visualising Ellen's delight when she saw—on paper—how perfectly appointed her home was to be.

She hadn't even been interested. Her letter made no mention of the drawings he had sent for her approval, not a word about the rose garden, the size of the upstairs rooms and the fact that he had pencilled in notes as to which he had considered would make the ideal nursery, the ideal playroom.

"And all for *nothing*!" he muttered savagely, almost, but for some strange unknown reason deciding against doing so, tearing the letter to small shreds and flinging them into the litter basket.

He rose and began to pace the room. He felt an urgent need to talk to someone, to someone who would understand how he felt and why.

Bob Anderson, the genial gynaecologist and his pleasant pretty wife Beryl had said, "Come round to us any time you like, Craig." That was when he had not been in Whemlybridge very long and had just purchased Grey Walls. It had been Bob who'd advised the gas central heating, Beryl who had talked so knowledgeably about the control one could exercise on the cooking, hot water and other domestic functions dependent upon heat. He hadn't gone round, he thought glumly now. He'd been to excited about having found the house, the precious and, or so he thought, important "well-established rose garden." He had talked—maybe boasted a little—of his plans and Ellen's, and now to go round and metaphorically cry on their shoulders, however friendly they might be, would be something he knew his pride could not bear to happen.

Sister Martha Dawson had been kind. She was almost

due to retire, and, or so he thought at the time, seemed inclined to take the new S.S.O. under her motherly wing. He had, he remembered, been a little impatient, simply because he knew Ellen did not like older women fussing around and telling her what to do! She always wanted to find out the whys and wherefores herself, and for that reason he had not accepted Sister Dawson's open offers of friendship.

He'd been on good terms with her, and with the rest of the staff, he thought wryly, but he'd made a friend of none of them . . . he'd been waiting for Ellen. She would be at home much more than he, and it was only fair to allow her to make the selection of the friends she would welcome to her new home when they were married.

But they weren't going to be married! That was a fact he had scarcely, as yet, allowed himself to accept. He ceased his pacing abruptly, knowing that unless he took himself from the confines of these four walls he might begin to smash something; he could feel the tension mounting inside him, and he felt he must get out and away, anywhere, where he could find someone to talk to, whether friend or complete stranger.

He had completely forgotten he had spent a long day in the theatre and that he had scarcely eaten anything since his breakfast that morning. He had drunk endless cups of coffee and of tea, but apart from a sandwich at lunchtime eaten in the doctors' self-service canteen, he had not eaten anything.

He flung out of the house, slamming the door shut behind himself, taking a kind of savage delight in the hollow sound it made as the noise echoed through the empty house.

With the same sort of gesture he pushed the key deep down into his pocket, his mind half toying with the idea of seeking some small hotel where he could dine, stay the night and waken to have breakfast ready for him in the morning.

The trouble was he didn't know the town well enough to know where he might find a small hotel of the kind he sought. He shrank from the "Gothic", where on odd occasions he had slipped in with one or the other of his colleagues for a brief drink. That was the only hotel he knew, and although there were doubtless countless others of equally sound repute, he did not feel inclined to investigate.

He unlocked his car, automatically glanced at the petrol gauge and started out, he knew not where. He drove round the town, staring now and then at lights in the windows of some of the houses as he drove past. In some of them he saw a man, or, hurtful sight, a man and a woman, she knitting, he watching television, but . . . together. In another house he saw children at play. Even as he drove by he felt he knew the tall man by the door with a small girl on his shoulder was the father, being welcomed home at the end of the day. He felt lonely and unwanted, and infinitely sorry for himself.

He drove out of the town and into the nearby countryside, but that was too unrewarding. He didn't know the area, and after a brief journey along darkened roads he turned a three-point turn and headed back for the lights and the people of Whemlybridge.

He drove down High Street without recognising where he was, and when he took a left turn and found himself in a cul-de-sac it seemed everything was pointing to him to stop. He got out of the car and locked it carefully, still feeling as though he had ben stunned, rendered senseless by some blow from which, as yet, he had not recovered.

There was a small opening leading out of the cul-de-sac and without any conscious thought as to where he might be going, he walked through it, finding himself in the midst of a crowded busy thoroughfare, with people coming and going as they left their work and went out and about on the evening's pleasure.

Craig saw none of them. Lost in his own miserable thoughts he strode along, hands thrust deeply into his pockets, looking neither to left nor to right. He looked across the road to where a flashing neon sign caught his glance.

"Book now for Christmas in the sun," he read. Suddenly it seemed like a good idea, and without thinking any more about it he stepped off the pavement and was suddenly aware of voices shouting, the sounds of brakes squealing and the sudden violent tug as someone took him by the arm and jerked him, with some violence, out of the path of the oncoming one-way traffic.

Although the last thought in her head when she had left the flat had been that she might see Craig Roper somewhere in the town that evening, Nona had felt no surprise when she had suddenly seen him apparently coming down the road. She had been standing outside the supermarket, her basket on her arm, concluding her conversation with Mike Robinson at the time, and, because they had been discussing the new S.S.O. she suddenly didn't want to be seen with the friendly porter. Hospital grapevines are a very real thing, and, in the mysterious way of grapevines Craig would somehow find out she had been discussing him—no matter how kindly or how matter-of-factly—with one of the porters, and she could well imagine his displeasure when such a story reached his ears!

"I'll have to go, Mike," she had made the excuse. "Nurse Foyly will be waiting for some of these groceries."

"O.K., Staff." Mike had grinned his customary cheerful grin as he lifted a hand in salute, turning on his heel and disappearing almost at once into the crowd, but Craig Roper came on! Abruptly he had halted, looked across the road to the travel agents on the other side, staring as though apparently mesmerised by the glowing colours of the light. The next second, without a glance to either left or to right, he had stepped off the pavement straight into the path of the swiftly-moving oncoming traffic.

Without pausing to think of possible consequences, Nona flung her basket to the ground, scattering the assortment of groceries right and left as she plunged through the milling groups on the pavement, to reach Craig's side.

There was no conscious heroism in what she did. She didn't even have time to think about it. She had literally flung herself from the pavement, disregarding the frantic sounding of car horns all around her. Instinctively she had grabbed him by his coat sleeve, just above the elbow. She had tried to take his shoulder, but he was much taller than she and it was impossible.

"Mr. Roper . . . *sir*!" she managed, holding firmly to prevent any sudden onrush into the traffic, since he did not appear to be aware, even now, of the danger in which he stood.

"There'll be a lull in a minute," she said, unconsciously adopting the tone she used when a patient needed to be soothed and reassured. "The lights round the corner should be changing any moment now, and that will mean the traffic this way's halted for a short time. We can get across then."

"I . . . do I *want* to get across?" he asked as though bewildered. "Why?"

"I thought you were going to the travel agency, sir," Nona ventured, but suddenly she was worried by the stunned look in his eyes, the shivering which seemed to shake him from head to foot, even as he talked to her.

"He's either been overworking or something has happened to give him a severe shock," she told herself, recognising the signs of undue tension in the eyes and round the firm mouth. At this point the traffic ceased to flow as, apparently, the lights around the corner changed to red, halting any further advance for the time being.

"Now!" Nona urged, abruptly conscious that for the first time in her history it was she who was suggesting to someone as important as Craig Roper the course of action he should take. Strangely enough he did not, as for one awful moment she had suspected he might do, appear to resent her action or her words. He stood before the window of the travel agents, staring at the colourful posters and pamphlets spread out as though in temptation, but he neither moved nor spoke for some minutes and, glancing at his set face, Nona had the sudden realisation that he wasn't even seeing the window or the display it contained.

"Your basket, Nurse!" She turned as someone she vaguely recognised as having been a patient at St. Jude's at some time or other, stood before her, holding the basket, her goods once more carefully packed inside.

"Thank you." She turned, wanting to dismiss the man, but he had taken a quick look at Craig's face although, thank goodness, apparently not recognising him. He wouldn't, she remembered. He was in Jude's before Craig arrived.

"Is your friend all right, Nurse?" the man asked helpfully. "I could help you get him to Maisie's Coffee Bar. He don't look too well to me!"

"It's nothing, thank you again," Nona said firmly. "We'll be getting along."

Obviously disappointed at not being asked to help further, the man said "good evening," but turned back to ask her to check and make certain he had recovered all her goods. A quick glance, as though she had completely memorised the list and could check by a single glance all were present and correct, had to serve to pacify the man who at last, with several backward glances at Nona and her companion, made his way down the street.

The lights, presumably, had changed again, and traffic

was once more humming through the highway. Nona turned to look at Craig. It was perfectly obvious he was waiting for her to make some suggestion as to where they should go next.

"Where's your car, Mr. Roper?" she asked quietly. "You didn't walk in to town, did you?"

"No. At least I don't think so," he said, frowning, his hands searching in his pockets until, abruptly, a smile of relief lit his eyes, making him look so much more familiar, so much younger and so much less strained.

"My car keys are in my pocket," he gave a short laugh, "so I must have driven down. It's stupid, I know, but I seem to have forgotten where I'm parked. I've never been in this part of Whemlybridge before this!"

"It's part of the old town," Nona was relieved to see the lessening of the lines of strain and tension, to hear the more normal note back in his voice and to observe for herself that he looked more like his usual daily self than he had done since she had first caught sight of him coming along the pavement. "When they made the new ring road this part of town took all the through traffic. That's why it's usually so busy this time of the evening. Local people, you know, either coming home from work or going out for a little pleasure," she concluded lamely.

"I see." He stood still, looking round. There were "No parking" signs almost everywhere he looked. Plainly he could not have left the vehicle anywhere easily within sight. He turned back to Nona.

"Where's the nearest car park?" he asked reasonably, "I suppose I might have left it there?"

"The nearest one is in Bolmoor Road," she told him. "The next nearest is the one by the market-place. Shall we try the one in Bolmoor Road first? We can get there this way."

He followed her without protest along the pavement and through a side-street a little further on. The side-street led into Bolmoor Road, but a quick glance along its length told him he had certainly never been there before. To make quite certain they walked along the rows of cars parked neatly in the allocated compound, but there was no sign of Craig's silver-grey and blue Rover, the one luxury he had allowed himself as a sort of personal reward for all the years of endeavour.

"I've never been in this part of the town in my life," he said firmly, so firmly that she felt a surge of relief. Whatever the cause of his strain and tension, some of it appeared to be wearing off. With a little more care, she told herself, he'd soon be himself again, but there was still that stunned look she didn't care for about his eyes.

"We'll try the market-place, then," she said cheerfully, wishing the shopping list had not been so extensive in the first instance and that she had not been foolhardy enough to augment it in the second place. The basket, carried some distance, was surprisingly heavy!

"Let me take that!" The authoritative note was back in Craig's voice, and Nona's heart seemed to skip a beat. That was another and almost sure sign he was returning to normal, as she thought of how he had behaved until a few minutes previously. She felt it was all wrong that she should even contemplate handing over the laden basket to Craig Roper, but when she hesitated he held out his hand, smiled faintly and uttered the one word "Please!" so that, still reluctant, she gave in and handed the basket to him to carry.

The public car-park in the market-place proved equally unrewarding. Nona frowned, trying to remember where there were others, when abruptly Craig caught her arm.

"It might have been through there," he said cautiously, pointing to where a small type of lane led off from the market-place and, as she well knew, back into High Street but entering it by the other end to that where the supermarket was placed.

"Couldn't have been," she said practically. "That

leads into a private park! Wait a minute and let me think." She wrinkled her brows, striving to remember from which direction she had seen him coming towards her, and suddenly she realised what must have happened.

"Where had you been, sir?" she queried. "Before you left your car, I mean?"

"I'm not sure." Craig spread his hands in a gesture of defeat to the grave danger of the contents of the basket. "I left the house and simply drove . . . I went along a road where there were a lot of fairly large houses." For a moment the stunned look was back in his eyes as he remembered the lighted windows, the families gathered together for their evening relaxation; the man watching television, the woman knitting; the man with the little girl on his shoulder, and abruptly the same lost and lone sensation which had descended upon him when he had first realised the contents of Ellen's letter, was back in full force.

"Then did you go along country lanes, where there were no electric light standards?" Nona probed, thinking hard.

"That's right!" Craig said in relief. If this girl, whoever she was, recognised the place from his vague description, then he could not have wandered so far away from Grey Walls after all.

"I know you, don't I?" he said suddenly. "You're at St. Jude's. You work in the theatre, but I don't remember your name."

He had never, Nona realised vaguely, called her anything else save "Staff." Perhaps he had never been told her name, not even when he had first arrived, but she hardly thought Theatre Sister would have been so remiss.

"I'm Theatre Staff Nurse Hoyle," she said quietly. "Nona Hoyle. We've worked together ever since you came to Whemlybridge."

"Of course!" He sounded at once so confident, so much the self-assured S.S.O. she had believed she knew as well as anyone in St. Jude's *could* know him that for a moment she almost believed all was well with his world now, yet a second look and a more intent one, told a very different story. He was making a tremendous effort to behave as normally as possible, but the stunned look was still in his eyes and his old, confident manner appeared to have deserted him completely.

"We'd better walk back," she said quite calmly, all nurse now, "and retrace our steps to outside the supermarket. A little further on the street is Blower's Fold. It's a narrow thoroughfare which leads into the Cathedral car park. I think you might have left your car there, walked through the Fold and forgotten which way you'd come. It's always happening to strangers here. I suppose that's because it's a really old town, and people have to grow up around here to know where they are now all these alterations and so on have been made! This way. . . ."

She led him back to where she had been standing when she had first caught sight of him coming towards her, gesturing to the small opening a little further along the road through which she guessed he must have entered the street.

"Recognise this part?" she asked lightly, and no one watching her would have guessed the depth of relief she felt when he nodded.

"I remember the travel agency," he said vaguely, "but I don't know how I came to be around here in the first place."

"That's easy . . . I think!" Nona smiled, and led him to the exit from Blower's Fold by which, as she had guessed, he had entered the street. She took him along there and to the cul-de-sac known locally as the Cathedral car park, and it would have been hard to have said just which of them was the most delighted to see his familiar car parked there, just as she had expected.

"I don't know what to say!" he announced blankly.

43

"I feel a perfect idiot! My only excuse is that I haven't had a great deal of spare time to get around the town and find all these entries and exits for myself. I do hope you weren't on your way to anywhere in particular, Staff Nurse? I feel very guilty . . . and in your free time, too! Would you join me in a drink—or even a cup of coffee—somewhere before you have to go? Perhaps you know where we can find something?"

"My flat's not far away," Nona was astonished to hear herself say the words, and added hastily, "I share a flat in Bannister's Ryde, with another staff nurse. I could make coffee in a matter of minutes, and, even though I say it myself, it's far better coffee than we'll get anywhere else!"

He hesitated for only a bare moment, then nodded. Suddenly he remembered that this was the girl who had returned his watch to him, he remembered her eyes, large and bluey-grey, with abnormally long lashes which curled at the ends. He remembered her hair, too, the way it swung round her face, shining and free, when she hadn't been wearing her duty-cap.

"Thanks," he said briefly, holding open the door of the car. "There's nothing I'd like better, if you're certain I'm not being a nuisance or that your friend won't object?"

CHAPTER 4

UNTIL that moment, Nona realised, she had forgotten completely about Avice. As she sat beside Craig Roper in the lovely, luxurious car she found herself, not worrying about being seen driving with the S.S.O., as she would have expected, but worrying as to what attitude Avice would adopt when she showed Craig into the flat.

She preceded him up the wide stairs, inwardly praying that her flat-mate would not be in one of her frequent facetious moods, but to her intense relief she discovered very quickly she need not have worried. There was a note in Avice's neat handwriting, propped up beside the sugar basin.

"Gone to the flicks with Joan Benson," she read with relief. *"Don't worry about supper. We'll eat out. See you in the morning if I'm late getting in. Avice."*

"Hope you don't mind being unentertained," she said as lightly as she could, screwing the note up and flinging it away. "Avice has gone to the pictures with a friend. Shall I put the coffee on?"

"Please," he said quietly. "If it really isn't any trouble."

Nona shook her head, smiling. She indicated the most comfortable of the chairs, plumped up the cushions and switched on the rented television, remarking that if he didn't want to watch there was a record player, a stack of records, both classical and pop, and a radio.

"I won't be long," she promised, and after watching him adjust the set, turn down the volume and relax in the big easy chair which was her favourite, she turned to the small box-like room which was their kitchen and breakfast room combined, and started work.

Suddenly she wondered whether he had eaten, and went out of the kitchen to enquire. He looked somewhat startled by her question, and hastily she added that she hadn't had time to make a meal since she came back from the hospital, so that it wouldn't be any trouble if he happened to be hungry.

"I am, a little," he admitted, realising abruptly how true was that statement. "There isn't much time. . . ."

"I know," she smiled at him. "I work in Theatre too, remember! Won't be long," and she whisked back into the kitchen before he could object.

This wasn't the first time she'd been glad of Aunt Mary's practical lessons in housewifery. She opened the big store cupboard doors and took stock of the contents. There were small canned potatoes, carrots, peas. In the meat compartment of the shared large fridge downstairs she had some stewing steak. Avice always said she preferred her packaged curries and so on, but Nona had smiled to herself when she had watched how frequently Avice had a double helping of anything Nona made from the fresh foods she favoured.

"There ought to be enough fresh vegetables left as well," she told herself, trying to remember when she had last purchased some and knowing full well that it had been during the week and not at the last weekend, because then Avice had shopped, hence the superfluity of canned goods!

She sped to the basement where the huge commercial refrigerator, shared by all the people in the flats, was kept. She had potatoes, carrots, a small turnip and Spanish onions in plenty. On the shelf in the store cupboard she knew there was a small jar of home-dried celery and another of mixed herbs, and, her eyes gleamed, a package of suet too! She'd use the pressure cooker which had been Aunt Mary's present when she heard her niece was to live out from the hospital. It wouldn't take long to make a first-class stew with dump-

46

lings, she thought, and she'd follow it by some of the apple pie she'd made on her last free afternoon. There ought to be plenty left! Avice wouldn't eat it because it might add to her weight!

She stole a glance at him as she went back to the kitchen. He seemed relaxed enough, leaning back in the depths of the chair, watching the programme but without appearing too deeply immersed in the action. Hurriedly she made the coffee, put on the stew and carried the tray of coffee into the living room while the meat cooked.

"I've made a man's type meal," she said almost shyly. "I hope you'll do it justice, Mr. Roper!"

"I'll try," he promised, sipping at the coffee, only to place the cup back on the saucer for a moment and say appreciatively: "That's good! Just what I must have needed!"

"I always feel a little that way myself," Nona said companionably, "when I don't have something as soon as I get in. I went shopping this evening, though. . . ."

"It was a most fortunate thing—from my point of view—that you did!" Craig remarked. "I don't know how long I'd have been wandering around looking for my car. . . ."

He broke off abruptly, replacing his cup—empty now —on the tray with exaggerated care. Suddenly he turned to look directly into her eyes and the thought struck him that never, not in the whole of his life, had he encountered such a clear, innocent and confidence-inspiring gaze. All at once he knew that here, ready to hand, was the "someone" he had been seeking, someone to whom he could talk, tell what had happened to him and why he had behaved as he had done . . . and that this "someone" would respect what he had to say as being confidential and treat it as such.

"I was more than just lost, Staff," he said quietly. "I'd . . . had an upsetting experience, and it rather . . . set me back a little. I'll be all right now I've . . . got over

47

it. I'd have been all right then, if I'd known anyone in Whemlybridge to talk to."

"I don't know that I can be any real help," Nona said deprecatingly, "but it sometimes helps to just talk aloud. You know me, and there's no one to hear whatever it is you have to say. It's none of my business, I know, but if it'll help you to . . . just talk it out to yourself aloud, go ahead. I shan't repeat any word of it, I assure you!"

"I know you wouldn't," he said with unexpected fervour, knowing that was precisely what he had felt about her from the beginning of the evening. "What do you know of me, Staff?" he asked next, startling her by the question.

"That you're an excellent surgeon," she began slowly. "That you've become one of the most popular people on the staff of St. Jude's since your arrival. That you've bought that big house, Grey Walls, that lovely big house with the marvellous garden, on Oakfield Avenue, and that you're shortly to be married. . . ."

"That's just it, Staff Nurse," he said deliberately. "That was what happened to make me . . . feel so . . . lost," he ended lamely. "I had a letter from Ellen, my fiancée. She's . . . found someone else. She doesn't want to marry me now. . . ."

He broke off and Nona waited, glancing at her watch. It was time to add the vegetables and the meat stock cube to the cooker, and with a murmured excuse she hurried out and into the kitchen, completing her details of the meal she was cooking and giving him time, it seemed, to recover his equanimity. When she returned he was sitting back, almost relaxed once again, his fine hands resting lightly on his knees.

"That smells good!" he commented in a flat tone, then, almost as though there had been no interruption, he resumed.

"I'd sent her the drawings I'd had made," he said. "They were of the various schemes of decorating I'd had suggested to me. I followed all the ideas we'd discussed over and over again. I only wanted her approval before giving the men the signal to begin their work. She hasn't even returned the drawings, much less commented on them. She's not been to see the house."

"She's a nurse, isn't she?" Nona flushed, aware she was giving away the fact that this was so much she had heard on the grapevine, but apparently he didn't mind.

"Ward Sister," he commented briefly. "She's Women's Surgical at Emley General. We were there together, for years and years."

"A long time, in fact," Nona murmured gently as he paused, and as though her words triggered off his thoughts on the subject he suddenly began to explain how in his first year at Medical School he had made up his mind how his future should run. When he had met Ellen Drayton and they had fallen in love, it seemed he had found the ideal mate.

"Our ideas were the same, Staff," he said firmly. "She didn't want to start off in some poky little house, trying to make do on the minimum and putting off having a family until we were certain we could afford everything they'd be likely to need! Now," he was abruptly bitter again, "she says she's going to marry some Dr. Dearby or other. A man who's starting as a junior partner in a combined practice in Emley! I could have done that, years ago, but neither of us wanted things to work out that way, trying to specialise and to earn a living at one and the same time! We couldn't even have lived together! She couldn't have lived in with me at the hospital, and we certainly couldn't have afforded to have both of us share a flat or something, as a married couple outside! You know how it is."

"At least," Nona said softly as the bitter note crept back into his voice, "she hasn't married her new friend first and told you about it afterwards, or left it for someone else to tell you."

"No one would do such a thing. . . ." he began, but the look on her face halted the words before he could complete the sentence.

"People do," she said soberly. "I know they do, because someone did precisely that to me. I know too," her clear gaze sought his own and somehow he felt comfort and strength in her steady glance, "just how you feel. I felt exactly the same way, for a time. Life didn't seem worth living. But it was, and is," she brightened suddenly. "Now I don't even think about it."

The pressure cooker hissed comfortably in the kitchen and another glance at her watch told her it was time to turn out her completed stew into an oven-proof dish. She excused herself a moment, then carried in the appetising-smelling meal, placing it before him and serving him a generous helping.

Craig did full justice to it. Until he had smelled the delicious scent of the cooked meat and vegetables in the steam which rose from the dish as she carried it into the room, he had not realised how hungry he was, or how much he had missed the substantial meals he had been accustomed to receiving from the kitchens of Emley General!

"How did it happen?" he asked unexpectedly as, at her invitation, he passed up his plate for a second serving. Without direct reference being made to the subject she knew at once what it was he wanted to know.

"He was in his last year as houseman here," she said quietly. "He went on vacation. He was going to make arrangements for . . . our future home before he started as his uncle's partner. He went on a short holiday, to the Lake District, I believe. Fate or something arranged that a girl who used to nurse here and who lived as a child and adolescent close to his home should be holidaying at the same place. The first indication I had of . . . anything was a brief letter and a cutting from the local newspaper. They'd been married two days before he wrote to me."

"And you stayed at St. Jude's?" he asked, adding as she nodded, "You hadn't quarrelled or anything?"

"Never a wrong word," she assured him gravely. "We never even argued."

"I can't say the same about myself and Ellen," Craig's forehead wrinkled. "We've had some blinding rows at times, when she's wanted me to accept a different way of . . . progress. When she's said it wasn't worth all the sacrifices we were having to make, but she's always come round to the same point of view in the end, that it would be all very well worth while, once the beginning was covered. I felt—I know—my appointment at St. Jude's is the beginning of all we'd hoped for, all we'd dreamed about doing together!"

"Maybe that's what's going to happen this time," Nona said, trying to keep a hopeful note in her voice. "Trevor and I *never* quarrelled, as I've just said. It wouldn't have come as such a shock if we had! I'd have expected him to come . . . running back to me. Perhaps your Ellen wasn't feeling well. . . ."

She wondered, suddenly, what she was like, this unknown Ellen who'd seemed prepared to stand by him throughout the long years which she must have realised would have to elapse before they could share the kind of life they had evidently dreamed about together. Perhaps this was nothing more than a simple matter of a lovers' tiff, and because he was alone and in a strange place, because he couldn't take Ellen out and coax her back into his way of thinking as, perhaps he'd been able to on previous occasions, the thing had assumed monumental proportions.

"She has migraine," he said lamely, "quite often. She'd been off because of that only last week."

If things had been all right between them just a week or so ago, Nona reflected, perhaps this unknown girl was simply not feeling well; perhaps, as he'd been at Whemlybridge for more than three months now and to Nona's certain knowledge had only had one free week-end which he had spent, presumably, back in Emley, she too was feeling lonely and neglected and thought it time to make him aware of how much he depended—or how much she possibly hoped he depended—on her continued love and belief in him.

"Could you telephone her?" she asked hopefully, and saw his quick anxious glance at his watch.

"Not now," he said regretfully. "She'll either be on duty or in bed. I know Ellen, regular habits are part of her very life! You think she may not be feeling well? That perhaps she didn't like the idea of my selecting all these things without her being here? I think it's rather ... much myself! A woman should have the choosing of the kind of décor she wants in her home, don't you agree?"

"Usually," Nona said briefly. She wasn't certain, suddenly, what she thought of Ellen and even of Craig Roper himself. In any other man the manner in which he had behaved this evening would have betokened weakness of character, in her estimation, anyway. Somehow the same thing didn't apply to Craig. There was nothing in the least "weak" about him, she reflected. He'd been tired. Only those who'd worked closely with him in the weeks since he had arrived at St. Jude's could possibly know just how hard he *had* worked!

He'd been at a very low ebb when he'd opened his fiancée's letter, so much was obvious. He'd been hungry as well as tired, and it must have been a little depressing to have to return to an empty house night after night, to look after himself the first thing in the morning before starting on his busy round at the theatre, without anything else occurring to worry him further.

"More coffee?" she queried, reaching for his cup. "And home-made apple pie with cream?"

"Lovely!" he said simply. "You take me back to the days when I was at home and Mother always had something like that ready for all of us when we came in. Those were the days!"

She brought the pie and the bottle of cream from the downstairs fridge. With no fears regarding her own figure and any problems which might arise, she cut herself a generous portion as well as one for him.

"Tell me about them . . . the days you mentioned," she urged, sensing his need to talk, to rid himself of the shock, the horror which must have gripped him when he had believed all he was working towards, all he had hoped for, was to be lost before he had grasped its substance. "What is she like, your mother?"

"She's small, but very sturdy," Craig said softly. "She gives the impression that she . . . well, can't manage without a man about the place, and really," he laughed softly, tenderly, "she's far more clever and more able to look after herself—and others—than a good many men. She's independent. Too independent for her own good. She's honest and speaks her mind, but *not* in such a manner as to hurt people. She's what I've heard people say is a 'typical Daleswoman'. She was born in Eldale in Yorkshire, you know."

"Are you the only child?" Nona prompted as he ceased speaking, but he shook his head.

"Two brothers and a sister," he said crisply. "One brother is an ophthalmic surgeon in Bradford. One's a dental surgeon in Wales. My sister wouldn't have anything to do with the physical welfare of others, or so she said. I think she's as much involved, though in a different way, as the rest of us. She's a kindergarten headmistress in North Yorkshire. Some time this year she'll be married to the local head of the Senior School. Wonder who'll dictate to whom?" He made the brief, not really funny joke, and Nona smiled.

"And your father?" she asked after a prolonged silence

53

when he appeared to be lost in thought. He seemed to recollect his surroundings with a start.

"Dad?" he queried. "He's big business. Started with a one-man taxi service just before the last war. Owns a fleet of his own cabs now, *and* a fleet of excursion buses as well. Does a lot of continental tours and so on."

"You must always have been a busy, happy household," she remarked so quietly that he sensed the longing unexpressed beneath the few words. He looked at her sharply.

"Have *you* a family, Nurse?" he enquired politely.

Nona shook her head. That she had literally no one of her own save Aunt Mary and Uncle Jack had long been a source of grief to her, but it was a grief she had, over the years, learned to live with.

"No one," she said with a brevity which betrayed her hurt. "Mum, Dad and my sister and brother were . . . wiped out in a holiday plane crash some years ago, before flying became the safe and customary thing it is today. I should have been with them," she added, "but I was ill and unable to go on holiday that year. At first," she remembered, "I used to feel . . . sort of betrayed. I used to wonder why I'd been singled out to be left alone. Aunt Mary taught me that many things which are hard to explain have a meaning, if we'll only 'be still and wait to learn what that meaning is.' She always said too, that if one 'threshed about' and worried a great deal when things got tough, it only made things worse. It does," she added firmly. "I've tried it. I think, too, I've found out why . . . I was left."

"Why?" Craig asked the question with real personal curiosity. It interested him to discover this totally unexpected philosophy in this girl he scarcely knew.

"Because I'm so much like my father," she said simply. "He had a very strong will; he never wanted anyone to lean on. It wasn't until I went to Dr. Harris—he'd been our doctor for years—to ask about my training as a nurse, that I found out Dad had known he couldn't live long anyway. That's why he'd planned this wonderful holiday for all of us together. Something to remember," her voice went lower. "And I was the only one left . . . with *them* to remember. Mother would have died of heartbreak if *she'd* been left. I think the same thing might have applied to the other two, but they were so much younger than I that it's hard to tell. The main thing, as Aunt Mary says, is that because I'm so much like Dad was I could stand up to it all, and recover. I might not have managed it without her and her husband, though. They've been wonderful."

"I think you've had your share of being 'wonderful' too," Craig said in admiration. "How old were you when all this happened?"

"Seven," Nona smiled. "I'm nearly twenty-three now. It's all so long ago."

"And how long since . . ." Craig hesitated. It seemed cruel to say the word "jilted", but Nona had no such qualms.

"Since Trevor married Alma, right out of the blue, you mean?" she asked in a casual tone. "Just over eighteen months now. *That* was hard at first, because everyone here knew about it."

"And you stayed on?" The answer to that question was so obvious it didn't seem necessary to say anything, so she merely nodded.

"Someone once said 'Courage consists in equality to the problem before us,' I think," Craig said quietly. "You've certainly shown you have plenty of courage, may I say 'Nona'? I've always suspected my own sex to be the emotionally weaker one. I think," he smiled wryly, "we've proved that point . . . between us! I don't know what got into me," he resumed almost to himself. "I just felt all my work, all my plans, everything I'd hoped for —and all I'd achieved so far—had been in vain! I couldn't stay in the house alone, tonight, but I'll be fine

55

now, when I get back. Would it be any trouble, do you think, to make another pot of coffee for me before I leave? I mustn't stay much longer, or neither of us is going to feel much like the responsible work of the theatre if I do!"

"I'll be fine, anyway," Nona assured him, intending that he should not be unduly worried on her account. "I don't need a great deal of sleep. I usually manage on six or seven hours at the outside."

He made no reply to this beyond a slight smile, and, moving very quietly, as he still looked very tired and in real need of a rest, Nona went out into the kitchen to brew up the fresh coffee.

She thought about him as she busied herself over the stove. There was something so frank and friendly about him, she reflected. With the new post he held at St. Jude's one might have expected him to have been a little more stand-offish, a little more reserved. Instead he had obviously been confiding in her as he would only have confided in a close friend—or the unknown Ellen had she been as close to him as, in Nona's opinion, she should have been—and in some strange way she felt she had made a life-long friend.

"Don't be an idiot!" she told herself as the coffee came to simmering point. "That's the way to more trouble for yourself! You have to remember you don't intend to get involved, not ever again, and anyway, once his lover's tiff's a thing of the past, he won't even want to remember this little episode! Men don't! He'll have some silly idea that it shows him up in a bad light or something. As though any girl with any sense can't realise things get too much for a man, just as they do for a woman, at times. He was tired, hungry and lonely. That's all there was wrong. I think he ought to go and see his fiancée. Once they've had another talk and he can explain he wants her to have things exactly as *she* wants them, it's all sure to blow over and he'll be sorry he's ever confided any of it to me! I hope I can make him feel I'm not interested in . . . spreading gossip, that's all! He wouldn't remain my friend if he thought I might!"

She finished off the coffee, set a fresh tray and added a plate of small cakes she had made when she made the apple pie, then she carried the lot through to him.

She spoke gently, and he did not answer. Nona walked to stand before him and saw his weariness had obviously overtaken him now he had spilled out his problems to someone else. Gently she set the tray down on a small coffee table and picked up a book. She would read, she decided, until he wakened, then heat the coffee up again. She switched off the television and the centre light. Seated in the small, comfortable modern rocking chair, the table lamp behind her, she could read in comfort and keep an eye on him as he slept.

CHAPTER 5

AVICE was thoroughly enjoying her evening out. She wasn't really greatly fond of an evening with one of her own sex, but there were times, she had discovered, when it was better policy to go out with one of the other members of the staff rather than to hold out for the invitation she really wanted.

Avice was a flirt and gloried in the knowledge. Throughout her career at St. Jude's she had achieved quite a name for adding scalps to her belt, and it was seldom that she was seen out with the same man on more than one occasion.

Her current target was the young R.M.O. who had been at St. Jude's only a little time longer than Craig, but Ron Adamson had a taste for the girls which rivalled that of Avice for men friends. She had angled for an invitation out from him for weeks, and when Joan Benson had called and explained that she had "accidentally" overheard the R.M.O. and one of the housemen making a date to go to the pictures together because it was too late to organise anything with any of the girls, she had readily fallen in with Joan's plan to stand in the cinema queue which formed every night since *Dr. Dolittle* had at last come to town.

It had been, after all, comparatively simple. They had walked the length of the queue slowly, taking care first of all, to make certain the two doctors were standing about a third of the way from the doors of the Palace. Standing on the far side of the road, pretending to study the new winter fashions in "Lucille's", it had been an easy matter to study their exact location through the mirrors in the back of the dress shop.

Two couples before their target, Joan had accidentally caught Avice's shoulder-bag strap, pitching the contents haphazardly over the pavement. Unitedly Ron and Peter Hale dived to retrieve the lipstick, the mirrored compact, with the mirror fortunately unscathed, the stick mascara and the box of perfumed face fresheners and a number of other odd items which managed to roll or slide into the most awkward corners possible. Avice and Joan had stooped too, and when they all four raised their heads to pool the recovered possessions, they were all laughing at the comical scramble which had resulted because at that precise time there was a change in the programme so that several seats were left vacant and the queue began to move forward.

"You're Women's Staff, aren't you?" Ron's hazel eyes were dancing with merriment as he asked the question, so that Avice was never quite certain whether he really remembered her or not.

"That's right," she said composedly. "This is Staff Casualty, Joan Benson."

"Were you joining on the end?" Ron asked in a low voice, not wanting the others behind in the queue to hear. Avice nodded.

"Wait in the foyer, then," he suggested. "We'll get your tickets. O.K.?"

"O.K.," Avice agreed. This was better than she had hoped for. She and Joan had planned to discover where the two were sitting and seat themselves as near to them as possible. Perhaps Joan's accidental catching of Avice's handbag strap hadn't been quite the unexpected event it had appeared to be! Mentally Avice saluted her companion; this was something she ought to have thought of for herself!

The foursome had thoroughly enjoyed the programme and when, as the National Anthem was being played, Peter suggested they all adjourned to Dino's, a small Italian restaurant which had just opened, they agreed.

Avice insisted, however, knowing it was a long time to next salary day and that the two young men might well have many other commitments to meet with their inadequate pay cheques, that they "went Dutch."

It seemed to have been the right move to have made, for over coffee at the end of the meal, plans were made for another foursome the following week, and when they left Dino's it was Ron who walked with Avice to where his car was parked, and Avice he placed beside him in the front passenger's seat. They had been driving along Lee Lane, a long way back to town, but, she reflected, a pleasant run, when Ron had remarked casually that this was much more sensible than "fixing up a home for a girl who doesn't seem to care where she lives or what the place looks like."

"You mean like the new S.S.O.?" Avice had asked innocently, her green eyes wide open to their fullest extent. She realised quite well his intention to convey to her that he had no serious intent towards "settling down" as yet. That suited Avice quite well. She wanted a few more years of freedom for herself as yet, freedom to date whoever took her fancy, freedom to flirt as and when she wanted, not to be tied, by bonds however light, to any one man, not even to Ron Adamson!

"Who else?" Ron drove the car off the roadway a little way and switched off the engine. Avice nestled against him as his arm came around her shoulder in a very experienced fashion. This was the sort of thing she felt she understood, providing it wasn't taken too seriously! *That* could well be left for much later, when she'd decided she'd had enough of hospital life and was ready to settle down!

They fell into light, general talk of the people who made up the staff of Jude's, of the current love-affairs about which everyone knew and the few which were only suspected and therefore the more exciting.

She was delighted to find her suspicions of Miss Redfern, assistant to Bob Anderson, known to all and sundry as "the gynae man," was known at present to be the almost constant companion of Stuart Mead, the portly, middle-aged pathologist. It wasn't clear as yet, Ron told her, just who was giving who the run-around, but he, Ron, would take level betting neither of them were serious!

"Doesn't do to get too set in one's ways in our profession, do you think?" he asked lightly, taking a long strand of her fiery red hair and winding it gently around his fingers. "I mean . . . take that friend of yours, Staff Theatre. She's a real example of what happens if one gets too fond of someone and then is let down! She never looks in the direction any of us happens to be walking, let alone comes anywhere we might be! What's she like to live with?" he probed curiously. "Cold, I should imagine. Peter and I had thought of asking you two out some time ago, but she looks through all the male staff, not at 'em!"

"She's O.K.," Avice said, and meant it. "She was . . . badly hurt, and she doesn't intend to get involved again."

"That doesn't mean she has to live like a nun!" Ron expostulated. "You don't!" and on his receiving an instant confirmation of that opinion the remainder of the evening went by very agreeably.

Joan lived in at the Nurses' Home, so the car dropped Avice off first. Clearly that wasn't exactly acceptable to Ron, for, as he leaned over to open the door for her, Avice heard his whispered suggestion that it might be a good idea to make it a twosome next time.

She felt she was walking on air as she ran up the stairs to the flat. Any new love affair had this sort of effect on Avice, and she quite failed to understand why Nona managed to remain aloof from all the twosomes, the foursomes, the excursions and the outings the others arranged for themselves. Nona, she had decided on more than one occasion, was missing a lot in life! Some-one ought to remind her she wouldn't always remain young and lovely and fresh-looking as she did now! Someone, Avice told herself as she tried the door and found it locked, ought to make Nona read whatever the poet had said . . . something about "gathering the roses while ye may, old time is still a-flying."

Perhaps it was the wine she had drunk at Dino's: it certainly hadn't been like any other wine she had ever tasted in her life before. She felt as gay as she always did after any evening's entertainment, no matter how ordinary, but, she giggled, this was the very first time she'd had trouble fitting her key into the lock! Surely, unless she had taken one of the small, innocent sedatives she took occasionally when the day's work had been too hectic, Nona must have heard her singing as she ran upstairs! If she hadn't heard the singing she must be deaf if she hadn't heard the silly sounds she'd made trying to get the key into the right place!

Nona had indeed heard her flat-mate's return. She had heard the car stop just below, the slam of the door and Avice's high voice calling "good-night." Tentatively she had touched Craig on the arm, and, as though in re-sponse to a night call, he had opened his eyes instantly, a puzzled look entering them as he realised he was in strange surroundings. Avice's somewhat noisy ascent of the stairs seemed to rouse him completely, but he sat perfectly still, watching the door, as they listened to her fumbling with the key. Nona was on her feet and half-way to the door as Avice swung it open. Craig had not moved.

"I've been with . . . Oh!" Avice halted, her eyes sending a series of searching glances from Nona's face to Craig's, to the tray still standing on the coffee table, the cups and the cakes all ready.

"You've had company!" Avice said unnecessarily. "Any coffee left?" she added with a touch of insolence which made Nona's heart ache. She understood Avice when she was in this mood, but, she felt, so very few other people did! Everyone else tended to think of her as a too-gay, too irresponsible person with no thought of the responsibilities of her profession, but Nona knew she was not in the least like that really. Avice wanted fun from life, and she saw nothing wrong in going after whatever fun presented itself, because, as she so often told Nona, it relieved some of the strain she felt when she was amongst sick people all day, people who ought to have been out and about enjoying themselves as she had been doing, and were, instead, tied to a hospital bed, and as often as not, in pain.

"There's plenty of coffee," Nona said quietly, hoping a cup of the strong hot liquid might help her friend to present herself in a better light. "It requires reheating. We've been talking," she felt she might be forgiven the white lie, "and it's gone cold. I'll heat it and bring another cup."

She hurried into the kitchen, leaving the door ajar. In this mood no one, least of all Avice herself, could imagine what she might say next! There wasn't long to wait before Nona realised the worst of her fears were to be realised. Avice had been intrigued by the new S.S.O. from the first day of his arrival, and like so many of the other girls on the staff one of the most intriguing things about him so far as she was concerned, was his complete disinterest in herself or any other member of the nursing staff, his total absorbtion in his unknown fiancée and the house he was preparing for her arrival.

"Did you come for some home-making hints . . . sir?" Nona heard the cheeky question. She could well imagine the gleam of mischief lighting the green eyes, the way in which Avice would toss her red hair as she awaited his answer. With all her heart Nona breathed a silent prayer that Craig, understanding person as she felt him to be, would be sufficiently understanding to realise this wasn't the real Avice talking, this was an Avice excited by her evening out—probably in the company of some new boy-friend, one she'd particularly wanted to go out with—and, perhaps, a glass or two of unaccustomed wine! Nona knew her friend could never resist sampling anything new and unaccustomed in the way of eating or drinking in any of the numerous small, attractive restaurants of all nationalities which had sprung up in and around Whemlybridge since the town became an over-spill area from the heavy industries area further north.

"Not exactly." She heard his deep voice with a sigh of relief. So far there was nothing in his tone to suggest he was angered by Avice's familiarity. "I . . . lost my way," he went on to explain. "Your friend Nurse Hoyle found me wandering around—in fact," the note in his voice deepened, "I'm almost certain she saved me from probably death or serious injury on the road. I hadn't realised I was in a one-way street and almost stepped in front of something. I suggested a coffee, and somehow," he sounded amused, Nona felt, "I found myself here, enjoying the best cup of coffee I've had since I came to Whemlybridge."

"Such a pity I'd gone out!" Nona could have yelled a warning to Avice, but she did not dare. She knew quite well the girl was intending to try his patience further. In the morning—or maybe later tonight, when she'd had her coffee and the effects of the wine had worn off a little—she would be sorry, but by then it would be too late! There was nothing she could do, however, so she gritted her teeth and prepared for the worst.

"It really didn't matter," Craig was saying evenly. "Perhaps next time I call you'll be at home too! As it was, I've had a most pleasant and restful evening. I've. . . ."

"I mean," Avice said deliberately, "if anyone had seen me go out and then saw Nona bring you home . . .

well, Matron would have something to say about *that*, wouldn't she?"

The coffee was on the verge of boiling, and with more haste than she would normally have employed Nona poured it into the coffee pot, spilling a large amount in her hurry. She didn't pause to mop up the mess, as she would normally have done. She was too intent on getting into the living-room and preventing Avice from saying anything else which might be even more disastrous than what had already been said.

"There's no necessity to talk that way, Avice," she said sharply. "Mr. Roper had received a shock." So much was the truth, anyhow! "I thought a cup of hot coffee and a little rest would be the ideal treatment!"

Deliberately she had omitted to say how long he had been with her, or that this was the third lot of coffee she had made! She was only thankful that, seeing him alseep, she had washed up after their joint meal and cleared away everything but the apple pie and cream and small cakes before settling down with her book. Wondering why Avice had not commented on the presence of his car outside the flats, she realised it was more than likely Avice had been too filled with happiness over her own evening out, to even notice it standing there! She was recalled to the present by Avice's next comment, spoken as she accepted her coffee, a comment which proved she had no thought of even attempting to understand!

"Mr Roper may well have received a shock, love," she said with exaggerated calm, "but that's nothing to the shock Matron would have if she thought one of her staff nurses was entertaining the S.S.O. in her flat . . . alone! I wonder," she drawled deliberately, "what your fiancée would think, sir? Don't you think she might object too?"

Nona's anxious, almost frightened glance sped to Craig's face. She had never seen him angry before, but there was no mistaking the emotion which showed so clearly in his eyes, in the tightening of the muscles round his mouth and the way in which his hands, resting on the arms of the chair, clenched suddenly.

"I fail to see that that's any concern of yours, Nurse," he said in a clipped, sharp tone. "Nurse Hoyle did what she could to . . . help me, just as I'm certain she would have done for anyone in like circumstances. I am quite certain Matron would understand *and* approve, and if you think otherwise, since obviously you appear to believe yourself in her confidence," there was a heavy note of sarcasm there, "perhaps you will do me the courtesy to wait to tell her your own, imaginative version of this evening, until I've explained to her precisely what *did* happen and why I'm so grateful to your friend?"

Perhaps it was the sharp tone, a tone no one in St. Jude's had heard him use before this, or perhaps the two swallows of hot, strong coffee she had taken had given some magical, instantaneous effect, Nona could not make up her mind.

Whatever the reason it seemed Avice was suddenly aware of the harm she might be doing, not only to herself but to Nona and to Craig Roper as well. She flushed scarlet, setting her cup down on the table with fingers that shook a little despite all her efforts to control them.

"I wouldn't go to Matron," she said sullenly. "Nona'll tell you that! I'm not that kind of a girl! I wouldn't get Nona into trouble for anything, she's had enough bother already!"

Nona felt the colour rush into her cheeks at this oblique reference to her brief and disastrous engagement, but she said nothing. Instead she stood silently drinking her own coffee and hoping Avice would have the good sense to go to bed almost immediately, but Avice had not finished what she intended to say!

"I'm not saying I wouldn't tell your fiancée, though,"

she said, speaking directly to Craig, apparently having completely forgotten he was the S.S.O. and that she should at least be respectful! "I don't know her, not personally, but the girl I've been out with tonight—Joan Benson—does. I'm sure she'd be . . . interested to know there's someone here in St. Jude's willing to keep a friendly eye on and to offer a friendly hand to you!"

Craig's patience seemed to give out with startling abruptness. Perhaps, Nona thought afterwards, it was the mention of his fiancée which could well have brought back the lost and painful feeling under the stress of which he'd been labouring when they met. She could remember only too well, and too painfully, exactly how she had felt when someone unexpectedly mentioned Trevor, even long after he was married to Alma!

"That will do, Nurse!" he said with some authority, rising and placing his cup on the table with a hand which was perfectly steady. "I think you would do well to remember that it's hard to decide who do the most mischief, those who are one's enemies and have the worst intentions, or those who call themselves friends, and have the best! You say Nurse Hoyle is your friend. In that event," he turned quietly away, "you will say precisely nothing of this evening, not to Matron, my . . . fiancée or to anyone else. I'll bid you both a very good night!" and with almost a formal bow to Nona, ignoring Avice further, he turned to leave.

Nona flung one glance in her friend's direction, a glance which she hoped expressed all the disgust, all the anger and reproach she could not put into words just then. Quickly she followed Craig to the landing outside the door of the flat, lowering her voice because of the occupants of the flat opposite and the fact that Avice, she knew, in her present mood would not be averse to listening behind the door.

"I'm sorry, sir," she said briefly, venturing a slight smile. "Avice isn't like this normally. She's . . . a bit headstrong, likes a good time when she's off duty, but she wouldn't deliberately hurt anyone, not anyone at all."

"She's the sort of person who keeps the grapevine going," Craig said with real bitterness. "There are, unfortunately, two or three of them in every hospital, perhaps in every large concern where the two sexes are working together. I wouldn't have spoken to her like that, but if Ellen's already upset. . . ."

"I'll talk to Avice later," Nona promised. "She doesn't mean any real harm, I know, and she knows me well enough to realise that my caring for you was genuinely because you were . . . in distress. There's no reason for her to know anything more than I've said in front of you; that you were lost, almost run over and had therefore received a shock. When she's been to bed she'll see the whole thing in a very different light."

"I hope so, for your sake," Craig held out his hand. "I seem to have caused a certain amount of disruption in your home life, Nurse! My mother would say that isn't the way to get myself invited here again."

"Of course you may call," Nona's fair skin turned a deep, rosy pink again. "Any time you wish. I don't go out much. I usually spend my off duty either sewing, reading or cooking! I'm not a stick-in-the-mud," she added, laughing as she saw his look of incredulity. "I like doing these things. They were part of Aunt Mary's philosophy of living, to be busy in leisure as well as at work, and to be busy with something useful!"

"And an excellent philosophy too, if I may say so!" Craig commented. "Thank you, Nurse. I shall remember that open invitation. Anyhow," he turned suddenly, "I'd like to come in and tell you what happens when I go to see Ellen . . . if you don't mind?"

"I shall look forward to hearing everything's all right between you both again," Nona said, and meant it, adding with a reassurance she felt he must be needing,

"I'm sure it *is* going to be all right, too. I have a feeling that way!"

"Then I hope you're right," he said quickly, "even if the way isn't as straightforward as it may seem!" With which cryptic remark he lifted his hand in salute and ran lightly downstairs. Seconds later she heard the sound of his car starting up, and nerving herself not to be openly angry, she turned and went back into the flat.

Avice was twiddling the controls of the television set and a blast of sound greeted Nona as she opened the door. Avice glanced round and saw her companion's set face, and without a word being spoken between them she switched off the set and faced the other girl.

"Sorry," she said gruffly. "I've behaved abominably, haven't I? It really wasn't intentional, believe me, love! It's just . . . well, anyone in trouble, anyone with any sort of sob story can get round you, and you've been hurt badly enough already. I don't want you to pile up any more heartache for yourself, Nona! Do remember the man's soon going to be married!"

The coffee, Nona thought abstractly, seemed to have done the trick. Avice was talking quite sensibly now, and apparently was quite sincere in what she said. Nona knew her friend had battled fiercely on her behalf when news of Trevor's marriage had become known, and she could quite believe Avice was only trying to shield her, Nona, from future hurt; if only she hadn't gone the wrong way about it!

"They've quarrelled," she said briefly, "and *that* piece of information isn't to go any further unless he says so! He's going over to see her as soon as he possibly can, and then, I expect, he'll bring her back here and he won't want to do that with any sort of story about the two of them going the rounds! It'll be a storm in a tea-cup, I expect. Everyone gets them, and it seems such a pity when he's bought that house and everything! Still," she began to clear the cups, "it's none of our business. I'm

only glad I was there when he stepped off the pavement!
He's a good S.S.O. and we don't want to lose him! Just
as you're a good staff nurse," she smiled to ease the sharp-
ness of her words and tone. "We don't want him to
retaliate—as he could well do if you did as you say—
by telling Matron just what you were like when you
came home! That wouldn't sound very well, either,
would it? And I know whose word Matron would prefer
to take, yours or his!"

"Don't be so self-righteous!" Avice protested. "Just
because you won't go out and have fun yourself! Don't
begrudge it to those who will and do!" She paused a
moment, then, with one of the impetuous movements
which endeared her to more than Nona however reluctantly, she flung herself at her friend.

"I'm a beast!" she accused herself angrily. "It's as
well you know me, maybe even better than I know
myself! I'm sorry, Nonnie. I won't say anything else, and
you're welcome to have the S.S.O. in for coffee and
comfort any other time you find him on the point of
committing suicide!"

Nona smiled, hugged her and refrained from the comment that no one had even suggested that idea might
have been in Craig's head. They made hot buttered
toast and, as a personal request from Avice, a jug of the
milky cocoa she always liked as a "sleep-drink," then
went to bed. Avice, Nona knew, was soon asleep. She
could hear her rhythmic breathing through her partly
opened door within seconds of her getting into bed, but
Nona lay awake a long time, staring wide-eyed into the
soft darkness, and seeing Craig Roper's face wearing
that dreadful blank, stunned expression it had worn
when she had first seen him advancing towards her on
the pavement outside the supermarket store.

CHAPTER 6

WITH obvious reluctance the warm golden days of
September slid gradually into October. The fine weather
gave way to a spell of wet, grey days which seemed more
appropriate for the approaching later November, but, as
Avice remarked one morning towards the end of the
month, at least they might yet have St. Martin's summer
to look forward to!

"I don't think so." For once it was Nona who was
being gloomy. "Once September's gone it seems to be
no time at all before we're helping decorate the wards
for Christmas. Don't you think, too, that any approaching festive time seems to send up the sickness and accident rate with an abnormality which seems almost intentional?"

"You're thinking of those kids in the alley down the
road, aren't you?" Avice queried, smiling sympathetic-
ally. "I know how you must feel, every time one of
them's brought into theatre, but don't forget we see a
large number in Casualty that you never even get as
far as the theatre, and some of them are in a pretty bad
way. They keep talking about some sort of legislation to
control this sort of thing, every Bonfire Night that comes
round. They talked about it when I was a child, and
still folks go on buying dangerous fireworks and letting
kids set them off without proper adult supervision! It's
always a wonder to me that more children aren't burned
or injured, despite all the warnings!"

"I suppose," Nona adjusted her cap and glanced
round the kitchen to make certain everything was safe
and in good order, gas turned off, electricity switched
off, taps not dripping, "it's because every year there are

more children coming up in the age groups that are interested, intrigued almost by the sight of the coloured lights, the crackle of an open fire and the pseudo-drama of the burning of a figure supposed to resemble that poor unfortunate man, Guido Fawkes! Poor chap, little did he guess that what had obviously started out in his own mind and those of his companions as a good idea, would, down the ages, degenerate into a sort of high-day and holiday—and a dangerous one to boot—for all the kids of the nation!"

"It's not only the children," Avice commented as she slammed the door shut and they walked downstairs together. "The grown-ups are just as bad! Take the man who came into Cas. last night! I bet he's not so happy this morning. His eye looked in a pretty bad shape when we sent for the R.S.O. I should imagine our friend Mr. Roper has had some pretty caustic comments to make about the large number of accidents we've had so far, hasn't he?"

"Not to me." Nona answered with her customary polite brevity as she always did when Craig's name was mentioned betweeen them. She didn't even pretend to understand him these days. So far he had been unable to get sufficient time off to see his fiancée, and, or so he had confided in Nona, first Ellen had been ill with influenza and had forbidden him to go and see her, even if he managed to get time off, for fear of spreading the infection.

After that Emley had been attacked by a mysterious virus which had filled the hospital and practically isolated the nursing staff. Barrier nursing had been set in operation, and Ellen, whether she had volunteered to do so or not, had been one of the Sisters in charge of that particular ward.

There was only one small grain of comfort, or so Craig had told Nona when they had met, by his arrangement, to go for a brief drive so that she could show him some of the beauties of the surrounding countryside, and that was that her proposed wedding date had been put back to early December. Matters between his late love and her new fiancée didn't appear to be progressing at the speed Ellen had obviously expected them to progress, and Craig ought to have been much more cheerful than he had been of late!

For herself, she reflected as the two of them descended from the bus outside the gates of St. Jude's, she had nothing to complain about. He was courtesy itself in the theatre and out of it. Added to that, he had twice invited her to go for a drive with him, and had behaved as circumspectly as she would have expected him to behave on both occasions. He had been to the flat on a second visit, when they had encountered one another shopping, and, her lips moved in an amused smile, she had been able to introduce him to one or two easy meals which he could well manage to do for himself!

Yet the fact remained that since the night he had received Ellen's letter, Craig Roper had been a changed person. He no longer walked, as Mrs. Lom had once said of him, 'like he owns the earth.' He no longer smiled at everyone, or cracked a joke with Mike or any of the other porters. He worked as efficiently as ever, spared himself nothing, but all the time there was that air of tension about him which betrayed itself in a thousand little ways to those who, as Nona, were watching for it.

"Did you know the Lamberts were moving out of the flat opposite?" Avice's words broke in on Nona's musings. Avice always appeared to have a fund of knowledge about everyone in the huge block of flats, but it was always Nona for whom any of the inmates asked if they were in trouble of any kind.

"No," she said now as they parted to go their separate ways to their own departments. "He must have got that job in Australia he wrote after. Whether they like it when

73

they get there or not," she joked as she shook her rain-hood before passing into the hospital doors, "at least they'll have sunshine! Who's coming in their place? Anyone we know?"

"They haven't even given their notice as yet," Avice preened a little. "They haven't told anyone else. Only me. Elsie told me when I met her in the hairdresser's. Remember when I went for a trim? They'd heard that morning—from Australia, I mean—and I don't think she could keep the news to herself a moment longer! Don't let them know I told you. I think they want to give a farewell party when they know their sailing date, and surprise everyone."

"I won't breathe a word!" Nona promised. "See you!"

There was a fairly long list for Craig that morning. Sir Alex, the tetchy consultant, had a fairly long list of his own private patients as well, and that meant, Nona reflected, checking the theatre, that he would be in one of his usual irritable moods, prepared not to have a moment's patience with anyone or anything!

Trolleys set, Mayo table ready, gown drum ready. Gloves out. Her brain automatically checked as her eyes and hands made certain.

"Morning, Staff!" She hadn't heard him come in, but as soon as he spoke she knew there was something different about him, something more alive and alert than there had been since that fateful September evening.

"Good morning, sir," she smiled at him. They always followed strict etiquette in and around the hospital, although she had been a little astonished to discover how quickly they had fallen into the habit of Christian names after their first social encounter, if such it could be called!

"List a mile long—as usual," he commented cheer-fully. "Never mind! Day after tomorrow you'll have to put up with my junior for a whole day. That *is* November the seventh, isn't it? I mustn't get the date wrong!"

"That's right." Mentally Nona counted off the days. Bonfire Night tonight. Some of its not so happy results tomorrow, she did not doubt. Yes, the day after tomorrow would indeed be the seventh!

"Going places?" she asked quietly so that Sister Theatre didn't hear, although Nona knew she was straining every nerve to listen.

"To Emley," he said crisply, holding out his arms for his gown to be tied. "I'm going to see Ellen. She's agreed to see me in the afternoon. I don't know whether I'm glad or worried. Her voice over the phone didn't sound like Ellen at all, just a matter-of-fact tone which seemed to say I could please myself whether I went to see her or not! Anyhow," he cut short his own discussion as the commotion in the corridor outside heralded the arrival of Sir Alex, "I'll at least see her, be able to find out what all this nonsense is about! Yes, sir," he answered a comment from the great man. Sister moved. The first patient was wheeled in and the work of the day had begun.

It was late when they had finished. Sir Alex had been driven away in the comfortable Rolls he had adopted more or less as a symbol when he had first achieved the status of consultant. The theatre had been tidied, Craig had scrubbed and was almost ready to leave when he turned and smiled directly into her eyes.

"Seems ages since you came after me with my watch, doesn't it?" he said blithely. "I ought to have seen then you were the one person I've met who's ever looked after me since I left home! You'll go on doing it, won't you, Nona?" he used her name, although there was a junior nurse at the far end of the theatre, gathering up the soiled linen and placing it in the baskets. "I mean, even if things don't go as I want them to do, if I'm disappointed and there's . . . more trouble when I get to Emley, you'll be the same, won't you?" he asked, almost humbly.

Nona nodded. She didn't trust herself to speak just then, with a junior nurse, ears pricked and eyes watchful, not so far away.

"Of course," she said quietly, and wondered if she was being wise. Avice would have said she wasn't. "Don't allow yourself to get involved again, love," Avice had said. "Remember, he is going to be married! Madam only wants a fuss, it strikes me! She'd have opted out long ago if she'd meant to! She just wants to test her power over him, and he'll go running, you'll see! They've been going around together too long now for her to break it off just like that! You're so silly. You'll let anyone take advantage of your good nature! Cool off, love, before you get yourself involved—and heart-broken—all over again. You should take a leaf from *my* book."

Nona had agreed that Avice probably had the right idea and forbore to mention that it wouldn't ever be the right idea where she herself was concerned. She couldn't treat anyone as Avice treated all the men she ran around with for a time, then, just as they were obviously getting serious about her, dropping them and moving on to whoever next had taken her fancy!

Ron Adamson, Nona remembered, had lasted approximately one month. Accustomed as he was to dropping a girl when he felt she was getting too serious for his comfort, it had been something of a novelty to discover that in this case he was the one to be dropped first. Both Avice—because she had used the technique so often previously—and Nona, who had watched her friend do exactly the same thing with so many others, could have comfortably predicted exactly what happened. For the first time in his life Ron now found himself really deliberately chasing a girl, a girl, moreover, who was not even a Ward Sister, as he exclaimed more than once to Peter Hale. But there was something about the redhead which tormented him, tantalised him, or so he averred, and in consequence his car was standing before the flat most of his off-days, and several evenings or whenever he could persuade someone to stand in for him!

"Good!" Craig answered her remark with a smile, and only then did she realise just what that smile meant where she was concerned. Automatically she fought against the idea that it meant anything at all! She mustn't allow it to mean anything! Not ever again, and especially when the person concerned was a man hoping to marry the girl he had courted for so many years!

"Will you have dinner with me—my treat this time?" he suggested. "Over at that small inn you pointed out to me last time we went for a drive. What did you call it? 'The Falcon's Head', wasn't it? It looks a pleasant enough place, and you said you'd heard they did a good meal."

"So they do," Nona answered slowly, "but . . ."

"You're not going to give me the same nonsense Avice tried to frighten me with, about someone telling Matron one of her staff nurses had been seen out with the S.S.O., are you?" he demanded, half laughing, but suddenly she could not even smile.

"It really isn't funny," she expostulated. "Matron definitely doesn't approve of her nurses being friendly with the medical staff here. It's the same in most hospitals, as you'll realise. . . ."

Suddenly the enormity of what she had just said hit her like a physical blow. He and Ellen must have come up against the same sort of thing in Emley! Yet, despite all rulings, somehow or other they had managed to at least become engaged, and surely, her mind reasoned logically, they must have gone out together on more than one occasion!

"I do know," he said very quietly. "That knowledge hasn't really got me very far, has it? I ought to have thought . . . perhaps we can think of something when I come back?"

"Perhaps," Nona echoed faintly, but something forlorn in her tone must have reached his ears because he turned immediately and spoke again.

"On second thoughts," he said, not even glancing to where her junior still stood, "let convention go hang! I want your advice as well as your steadying influence tonight! We shall be rushed to death tomorrow, I suppose, and have no time to talk. I want you to advise me; tell me what line you think I should adopt where Ellen's concerned? Or, better still, come and look round Grey Walls and tell me if there's anything else you think I can do, sketch or suggest which might help."

"I couldn't do that!" Nona could not have said why, since ever since she had come to know him as a person she had wondered exactly what sort of house he had bought for his bride, what plans he had made, what ideas he had caused to be put on paper and sent to Ellen. "It . . . she wouldn't like it," she amended. "I just couldn't. . . ."

"I suppose not," he agreed instantly. "I was a clot to suggest it. My first idea was the best one, and the 'Falcon' is quite a way out of town—and not the sort of place many of the staff'll go to, I suppose?" he queried.

"No." Nona shook her head. "It's too expensive for most of us," she said, and wished she could have voiced even a hint as to the financial side of the arrangement, but he just laughed.

"I know!" he grinned. "That's why I think we might splash on this occasion. I'll pick you up at your flat around seven-fifteen, shall I? From what little I've gathered here and there it seems most of the children—and the parents—of Whemlybridge will be either occupied with their own private little bonfires tonight or taking part in the huge one the authorities are arranging over in Wheyland Park. I believe I've heard someone say there's a November the Fifth dance as well, although what anyone can find to dance about on such an occasion is more than I can imagine!"

"Probably a great deal more than the people could find to dance about on the first Bonfire Night!" Nona's sense of humour, never very far away, was returning. "History was never my favourite subject, but I seem to recall there was a good deal of Puritanism about, *and* a great deal of religious persecution. I wouldn't imagine anyone had much cause to dance! I know I wouldn't have had!"

"I don't know about that!" Craig said, unexpectedly. "How about it, then? Can you be ready by seven-fifteen?"

"Yes. . . . and thank you!" Nona didn't know why she had accepted. Feeling as she did now, even though as yet she hadn't faced up squarely to how she felt, it would be like twisting a knife in a wound, but that was something which was to come hours hence, not just now, when he was smiling into her eyes.

"See you later, then!" Craig said cheerfully, and went off, whistling softly, down the corridor. Nona glanced round to make certain all was in order and saw the junior hurrying to push the last of the soiled linen into the basket and wheel it away. She did not know how much the girl had heard, or what her thoughts had been, but it took a real effort of will not to rebuke her for being slow or to even suggest that she might have lingered in the theatre in the hope of hearing something which didn't concern her!

"That's the way shrews are made!" Nona told herself. "Judge not, Aunt Mary always says, and she's usually right!"

Memories of her aunt's teachings and words of wisdom always had a soothing effect upon her nerves, so she smiled at the girl, told her gently she would have to learn to move more quickly if she didn't wish to incur

Sister's wrath, and went off to the staff nurses' sitting room for a greatly needed cup of coffee.

Joan Benson was in the sitting room too, and Nona realised with a start that she ought to have expected this. Matron Frost had a healthy dislike of overworking any one of her staff, and so far, although the renowned Bonfire Day was only partly over, Casualty had been very busy !

"Taking a breather, Nona?" Joan enquired lightly, and, relieved that the question was in no way personal, Nona nodded.

"I hear the S.S.O.'s off for a day on Thusday," Joan chattered on. "Bet you'll miss him ! Sir Alex's promised to be on call if anything major crops up, I've heard. Otherwise you'll have to put up with the Surgical Registrar, and *he's* already modelled himself well and truly on Mr. Rawlingson, I hear !"

"He's a long way to go before he reaches *that* standard !" Nona commented, and hoped devoutly Joan wouldn't read that as a criticism of the Junior Surgical Officer, who was, on the whole, a very pleasant person although apt to get a bit flustered if the lists became crowded.

"Maybe." Joan rose, glancing at her watch. "Anyhow, you're welcome to all that lot ! Give me the comers-in and the goers-out," she laughed. "I'm no great shakes on the folks who are here for a long period ! I'd rather be where I am, or on O.P.'s." Nona remembered Joan had once asked to be Staff Outpatients and been annoyed because Staff Purgoose had been given the post instead. "I'm like Avice," she concluded as she went through the door, "I like variety ! Going to the dance tonight? Some of the crowd will be there. They've all got late passes. You're lucky, you and Avice both ! You don't need 'em. Providing you're in on time in the morning."

Someone else came in then and immediately began asking Joan about the party being made up for the dance at the Town Hall that evening. Nona took the opportunity to escape, wondering if she were ill to be imagining hidden meanings in almost everything anyone said.

"Time you took a hold on yourself—and on your imagination—my girl!" she said mentally, but all the same, changing into a hyacinth blue two-piece and a very fussy, frilly blouse of white chiffon which gave the whole outfit a festive air, she felt excitement rising inside her, and try as she would, it was impossible to hide it even from herself.

"Going places?" Avice unconsciously used exactly the same words Nona herself had used to Craig earlier that day.

"Just out to dinner," she said with as casual an air as she could summon to her aid. Avice eyed her in silence for a moment, then sighed.

"It's no use my saying anything, I suppose?" she ventured. "It's the S.S.O., of course?"

"Yes." Nona could have slapped herself for adding almost at once : "There are several things he wants to discuss before he . . . goes away."

"He's only going for the day, isn't he?" Avice prompted, "and I don't suppose much of what he wants 'to discuss' has any connection with St. Jude's or its patients?"

"I . . . I'm not certain what it is he wants to discuss," Nona said defensively, but with truth. Avice gave a brief laugh.

"I'd take a level bet it's something absolutely private," she said, continuing in a tone of genuine concern : "Don't take any of it too seriously, kiddo! Remember you've been hurt once . . . and I wouldn't say you'd altogether got over *that* as yet! Anyhow," she said reflectively, "I'd have said you'd taught yourself not to put too much trust in princes, or whatever the saying is! The S.S.O.'s no prince, but neither, to the best of our knowledge, is he a free agent! I'm not thinking of *him*."

The scorn in Avice's voice would have intimidated anyone who did not know her as well as did Nona. She knew the scorn was what she professed to feel for men in general although, as she so often remarked, "We can't do without 'em, but it's as well to know they're most of 'em, up to no good so far as we girls are concerned!"

"We're merely having a friendly meal and a talk," Nona said with a quiet deliberation which meant she was not prepared to discuss the matter further. Avice knew that tone of old. When Nona spoke like that it meant she had, metaphorically speaking, put her back against the wall and no amount of argument would sway her, not even a trifle.

"Good," she said briefly, her green eyes still watchful. "I shan't be in late myself. Have a nice time . . . see you later!" and before Nona could comment she was gone and running lightly down the stairs as Ron's car horn sounded outside the flats.

Nona hesitated. One half of her mind, the half which had been so badly hurt by Trevor Brady, knew Avice was right! She wasn't the type to love lightly, to enjoy a flirtation and be off and away to the next man in no time at all!

"I ought not to go!" she whispered to herself, but there was the sound of a man's footsteps running up the stairs—Craig never blew his horn for her, he considered it undignified, he said—and she knew she could not tell him she had changed her mind.

Pride and dignity were her armour all through the evening. It was much easier than she had anticipated, because of the simple reason that Craig had no idea whatsoever of the discovery she had made and only half examined, when he had smiled at her in the theatre when she had said she would always be the same where he was concerned.

Craig, she told herself, was thinking she would always

be the same confidant, the shoulder to cry on, the friend and adviser she had made herself the night he had received Ellen's letter, and that was not how she felt at all, she realised as she sat opposite to him in the beautiful candlelit dining-room at the "Falcon".

Craig chose the menu, choosing carefully all the things he had heard her mention at one time or another as being what she liked. There was a small orchestra playing what he referred to as "Palm Court type music," and it made the perfect background to conversation.

"This has been most pleasant," Craig observed, proffering a light to the cigarette she had just accepted. "I feel much better, much more able to counteract any objections Ellen might by this time have cooked up to our previous arrangements. We must do this again some time," and then as though Nona's eloquent blue eyes were a distinct reminder of the reason for this tête-à-tête, he added: "The three of us, I mean . . . *if* I can persuade Ellen to change her mind."

Nona was silent for so long he thought he must have offended her, but, gathering her handbag and gloves together, she prepared to depart. She felt she *had* to indicate that she was ready to leave. She couldn't have sat there much longer, discussing the everlasting subject of Ellen who, as portrayed by Craig, seemed a cold, self-centred individual.

"And if you can't . . . persuade her?" she managed at last in a small voice. "I suggest we don't repeat the experiment. It wouldn't be wise . . . not in our respective positions."

For a moment Craig looked at her as though he could not quite believe he had heard correctly, then he smiled.

"I won't even think of such a thing, Nona," he said forcibly. "Before I met you, came to know you as a friend, I might have agreed. Now," he smiled and her heart lurched, "I know you almost as well as I know myself, or I think I do! I was ready to accept what must have been a sudden whim on Ellen's part, or the product of her not being well, as we decided the night I'd heard from her."

"Did we?" Nona wondered in her heart, and, thinking back she could vaguely remember having suggested to him that perhaps when Ellen had written in such a fashion she had not been feeling well.

"If she had meant what she wrote," Craig continued, "they would have been married by this time . . . but they aren't. I had a letter from a friend of mine in Emley yesterday. He says there's some talk of David Dearby going abroad. He says he wants to emigrate, and I can't see Ellen willingly doing *that*! No," he said so complacently that she could have shaken him, "I'm a much braver, much wiser man now I've talked so much to you. I shall leave all the choice of decoration, of furnishing and so on, to Ellen when she comes. I shall book rooms for her, maybe here," he glanced round the pleasant public room, frowned and continued, "or maybe at one of the smaller hotels in Whemlybridge, I don't know. There's ample choice. I didn't realise that when . . . before I got to know someone here."

Nona felt she would scream. She had guessed it would be a trial of her own strength to come out with him on an intimate date like this, but she hadn't realised exactly what a trial it really would be!

"I ought to have known," she thought, only half listening as he talked on and on. "I ought to have realised why suddenly the theatre is the most wonderful place in the world, apart from all the miracles we see performed there daily! I ought to have realised what was happening when the day seemed brighter because he's been in for a chat as well as to work, but I *didn't* know, didn't guess what was the matter with me until he smiled that special smile. . . ."

"And I hope you two will be great friends," Craig was concluding some long sentence of which she had only managed to hear these last few words. "It'll be good for Ellen to have someone here she can know as a friend from the beginning."

"I . . . I wouldn't altogether count your chickens," she managed at last, rising so that he was bound to realise she meant what she said when she had mentioned that he would have a long drive and she a long day after this evening's oasis of relaxation.

"Maybe you're right," he said, pulling back their chairs, "but one thing I am sure of . . . whatever way it all works out it'll be for the best. It couldn't be any other, when you've been the one to sort of 'take charge' from that night on!" and those words were still going round in her brain long after he had been into the flat, enjoyed his coffee and said a final 'good night.' She went to bed before Avice came home, pretending to be asleep as she heard her friend's key in the lock. There was only one small comfort in the whole of the evening; if he really believed she had taken charge and done her best to help him decide to go and *see* Ellen with a view to making her change her mind, then her secret was safe. He didn't, she decided, turning over and burying her face in the pillow, know what she herself had only realised that day, that she was in love with him herself!

CHAPTER 7

NOVEMBER the sixth dawned grey and perfumed by the after-effects of the numerous bonfires and exploded fireworks of the previous night's activities. Authority had closed one eye to the contravening of the rules which governed a smokeless zone, just for the one night. Now police and firemen were patrolling the town and the outlying areas, checking that no danger lurked amongst the hot embers, some of them still aglow.

At St. Jude's, as at so many hospitals throughout the country, the Casualty department was busiest of all, but there was work in plenty in Theatre too. Craig whipped through the list as though possessed of the strength and endurance of ten men. A partial gastrectomy, a strangulated hernia, an emergency appendicitis : backed by Theatre Sister and her team he worked solidly until the last patient of the day was wheeled into the recovery room.

"That's it, Staff!" His voice was purposely loud for Sister and everyone to hear. "I'll be back bright and early the day after tomorrow," and for Nona's ear alone he added : "I *might* call around when I return. O.K.?" before resuming a louder tone to add : "See we don't have any D.O.T.s while I'm away, won't you?" and laughed.

She thought about that remark often during the evening, when, reluctantly, she was persuaded to accompany Avice to the nearest cinema, but she refused to repeat the experiment the following evening. She could not have said why, but she wanted the comfort of her own flat's walls about her, the solidarity of familiar things. Determined not to go out, she hurried for the bus prior to the one Avice was sure to catch, so as to be first in the flat and to try to compose herself for the evening which lay ahead.

Avice was home shortly afterwards, full of plans which included Nona should she agree. For some reason Avice had decided her friend required cheering up, but Nona shook her head, declining.

"No, thanks all the same," she said quietly. "I'm going to wash my hair, catch up on my letter to Aunt Mary and get that done before the film comes on the television . . . it's an old one, but I remember seeing it a long time ago, and I enjoyed it. Then I shall take a book to bed and read until I feel sleepy."

"Good for you!" Avice said unexpectedly, her glance appraising Nona as though she didn't really believe what the other girl had just said. "So long as you're not going to sit there moping because Craig Roper's on his way to see his one-time fiancée."

"Who he's hoping will consent to become his fiancée again!" Nona put in quickly, too quickly, Avice thought, her eyes narrowing.

"That's as maybe," she said cryptically. "I wouldn't mind betting he doesn't even call to see her! He's spent far too much time here and taking you around to be worrying overmuch about Ellen Whatshername! If he'd been as heartbroken as he *seemed* to be that night he first came here, he'd have been over to Emley before now, whether she was ill or not! What *was* the matter with him that night, anyhow? You've never really told me. You always seem to avoid talking if I try to bring the subject up at all! I know he's written no end of letters to her and that they all come back unopened. Mrs. Lom told Mrs. Davis who told. . . ."

"The cat who told the dog who told the man who brings the papers round the wards," Nona lost her temper—a most unusual thing for her to do with anyone, Avice least of all—and only by making a really supreme

87

effort did she regain control of herself sufficiently to carry on more normally.

"Why people in a hospital have to mind everyone else's business I always fail to understand!" she said decisively. "It's nobody's affair but Mr. Roper's own what happened to him that night! He'd been working hard, not just that day, but from the moment he came to Jude's. Gossip will allow him that much, I suppose?"

Avice nodded silently. This was the Nona she had known *before* the days of Trevor Brady's desertion. This was a girl afire with indignation, and this time it was not on behalf of some poor, ill-treated child or animal, or someone in one of the acute wards, very ill and in considerable pain.

This, she reflected, was purely emotional, and for Nona to become emotional where someone of the opposite sex was concerned was so unexpected that Avice, like the Bard, began to feel "the lady doth protest too much!"

"I know he'd been working hard," she said more quietly than she normally spoke, "and I bet he'd not had anything to eat before he left St. Jude's either. But for a man to get lost in a little town like Whemlybridge, and not be able to find his car . . . *and* he looked as though he'd either been asleep or had some sort of a shock when I came in! I wasn't quite myself, I know," she grinned, remembering, "but I do know I thought he didn't look the usual immaculate, urbane S.S.O. I'd been used to seeing round St. Jude's! Just what *had* happened, Nona? You didn't make a friend of him when you returned his watch. What was so different about this occasion?"

"He . . . he needed someone," Nona said simply. "He'd had a shock. He'd . . . his fiancée had written calling the engagement off. Maybe she'd got cold feet about the whole thing, maybe she just didn't like the sound of St. Jude's, or maybe she resented the fact that she hadn't been able to get over and see the house he'd bought for her before he'd put his signature on whatever documents are involved in such a transaction, I just don't know. They've been going out together for such a long time he couldn't believe it. He was like a man who's been poleaxed, or whatever it is. He was just . . . stunned. That's how he came to forget where he'd left his car, that's how he nearly got himself run over . . and if I hear one word of this over the grapevine that's the end of our friendship, the end of my shielding you from Matron's knowing just what you do in your off-duty *and* who you go about with more often than not. . . ."

"Steady, steady!" Avice laughed warningly. "I'll not breathe a word, I swear it! I must admit I've wondered why she's never shown up, never even come to see the house or anything. Poor old S.S.O., no wonder he was all of a doo-dah! But don't let him get you the same way! Wait until he comes back. We'll know then whether it's on or off. . . ."

"It will be 'on,' as you phrase it," Nona wasn't aware just how weary was her tone. "He . . . they must have been in love a long time," she said slowly. "They've known one another over five years, been engaged just over four of them."

"She can't claim to have been rushed off her feet at that rate, can she?" Avice asked with irrepressible humour. "She's either grown out of love with the idea, or she wasn't too keen in the first place! It's gone on too long, to my way of thinking. She's decided to be a career girl after all!"

"He wanted her to have . . . everything as *she* wanted it, right from the start," Nona defended him valiantly. "She wanted a house with room for a family. She wanted an established rose garden. She wanted him to have time to devote to his home, time for a life of their own as well as the time he would have to give to his career! It isn't easy for them, you know, Avice. Not for the men who have the ability—and the desire—to get to the top of the tree in medicine or surgery. They didn't want to. . . ."

"Struggle?" Avice put in as she sought for the right words. "Maybe they made a mistake, else they weren't really in love. If they had been, they wouldn't have cold-bloodedly planned like this. The minute he'd been earning a reasonable amount they'd have taken a chance, especially when she was working too! People in love don't weigh up all the pros and cons like that! It isn't human. It's too calculating. I think they were just attracted, and now she's grown out of the idea. It might be as well if he did the same thing, in my opinion!"

"He won't," Nona said flatly. "He's worked and worked hard, every exam he's taken has been as much for her sake as his. Every step of the way has been with a mutual end in view! Apparently everything was fine until he left Emley and came here. I suppose she felt lonely, missed him and all the rest of it . . . and as soon as they see one another again it'll all be as it was before."

Craig's thoughts had run along the same lines as he journeyed. He had turned into Emley, remembering so well the little road of select houses where Ellen had a small one-roomed flat and to which she returned on her free days and on vacations. Her normal off-duty was spent in the Nurses' Home, in her room in the Sisters' Wing, but when she had a forty-eight or a long weekend such as she had this week, this was her refuge.

He stopped the car outside the gate of number twelve. The same prim evergreen hedge glinted its prickly leaves at him in the light of the late November afternoon's weak sunshine. The same prim net curtain remained drawn against the glance of the curious, giving the house a blank staring look.

He rang the bell, and Mrs. Pollard, Ellen's landlady, came to the door. She bit back an exclamation of surprise when she saw him.

"I'll see if Sister Drayton is at home, Mr. Roper," she said gravely, but Craig merely smiled.

"I know she is, Mrs. Pollard," he said quietly. "I know that's her room with the sound of the radio playing. No one else round here listens to the Third Programme!"

She gave in then, and reluctantly opened the door to admit him into the straight passage-like hallway with the stairs rising from almost opposite the door. Her glance dared him to come one step nearer, and he waited, feeling oddly uncomfortable, under the stern gaze of the imitation marble bust of Beethoven which seemed to glower at him from the top of the hallstand.

"Sister says you're to come up, please." Mrs. Pollard come to the top of the stairs and stood watching him place his gloves on the hall table. "I'm to bring tea," she announced grimly, as though the prospect didn't please her at all. "Is it still strong and with two sugars?"

"That's right." Craig didn't care whether it was strong, weak or even non-existent. He wanted to see Ellen, to see if she was as he remembered her, and to find out just what had gone wrong between them.

She was exactly as he remembered her. She was tall, almost as tall as he was himself, her long hair smoothly parted and done in a sort of coronet on the top of her head. Some people thought the style old-fashioned, but it suited her. Her eyes, grave, dark grey and careful, looked into his own, and she held out one cool hand, for all the world as though he were a perfect stranger, he told himself.

"How nice to see you, Craig!" she said in her cool, pleasantly modulated voice. "You must be tired after your drive. Mrs. Pollard is making some tea."

"So I understand," he said crisply, but he did not sit down. He took one step towards her, and was amazed when she withdrew with equal rapidity, adroitly placing herself behind the table and out of reach of his extended hands.

91

"What's wrong, Ellen?" he said quietly. "Something is *very* wrong, I realise that, but as to what it is, I must confess I am really in the dark! You didn't say anything about not wanting to marry me when I left Emley! If you had, I should never have taken the job."

"That was why I didn't say anything," she said composedly. "That's why I've never said anything, not all these wasted years."

"Wasted years?" Craig was genuinely puzzled. These were the years in which he'd risen, step by step, to the post he now held, the stepping stone to a consultant's position in the very near future! Near, that was, when he remembered how long ago it was since they had first discussed their plans together.

"Wasted for me," she interrupted quickly. There was a flush in her cheeks and her eyes were bright, and altogether she loked a very different person from the cool, calm, always controlled Ellen he knew—or thought he had known—so well. "Can you remember how we talked on our first date?" she cried, and as he still looked bewildered, she shook her head.

"I knew you wouldn't remember," she said in a tone of accusation. "You talked about what we could do with our lives, where we could each get to . . . separately, because it would be too soul-destroying to start out together and to be poor."

"You agreed," Craig said, feeling suddenly helpless. "You know you did."

"After a time." She was suddenly the familiar, cool-toned Ellen again. "I don't suppose you'll remember that I said I didn't mind being poor, if we were together! *You* convinced me it would ruin whatever we felt for one another. You painted such glowing colours of what it would be like to be the wife of a consultant, how much better off we'd be financially *and* socially, and," she was suddenly bitter, "I allowed myself to be convinced! I was a fool!" She was abruptly passionately angry again.

"I ought to have known then it was more important to have a home and a family while we were young enough to enjoy them both! I didn't want the glory, only for you! Now," she spread her hands helplessly, "I shall find what I want . . . with David. It isn't too late for me to have a family, though I'm so much older now I shan't have the fun we'd have had together when we were both in our early twenties! At least I'll have them before it's too late, and if we're worried about school bills, clothes, holidays and all the extras that go to the raising of a family, all right! We'll worry our way out of it like the rest of humanity! At least we'll be living."

"We could do all those things *now*, Ellen," Craig said more humbly than she had ever known him to speak. "We can do all of them so much more comfortably . . . right now! This is what we'd planned. . . ."

"What *you'd* planned," she cut in. "I don't think we were ever meant to marry, Craig, not when I really think about it. If we'd been at all keen on the idea we'd have let the future go hang—except for working as we've both done all the time, and waiting, taking every opportunity, for something to develop which would help you get to where you wanted *and* be together as well."

"We've been together," he began, but she interrupted him quickly.

"Working in the same hospital, that's all," she contradicted quickly. "Sometimes, as you know very well, we didn't see one another privately for weeks on end! That's not what I call being together! I know it's been different for you. You'll make the top, I wouldn't be surprised if you don't end up in some select rooms off Harley Street before you've done! But I shan't be with you! And you won't really miss me," she averred. "You'll drop into the swing of things, choose a really beautiful, classy, socially-minded wife, and forget all about the dream we thought we shared. We didn't, you know," she went on more gently. "We were looking for different things and just didn't realise it. We'd grown accustomed to one another, but all the time you were looking towards an important future, and I was only looking for a home, a family and a man to come home to us all."

"I . . . I'd no idea!" Craig was genuinely astonished. "Why didn't you say so?" he demanded. She shook her head.

"When?" she asked simply. "On the rare occasions when we managed to be off duty together? It wasn't possible, when you had so many plans for our mutual future, and all of them, you believed without even asking, to be as important to me as they evidently were to you! It's no use, Craig, and I'm sorry, but it really isn't any use at all. You'll find someone else, and your heart won't be broken. Right now it's your pride that's hurt, just as mine would have been if you'd been the one to see it first!"

"I bought the house I thought you'd like," he began, feeling foolish. "It even has the established rose garden you said you wanted."

"And how much time do you think you'll spend in it?" she pressed the point ruthlessly. "That's not what I'm looking for, Craig, and you must realise this *now*, or you'll never understand what I mean."

"I thought you were happy," he began, but she interrupted again. In no way was she behaving as he remembered her!

"I'm happy now," she said with deliberate slowness. "David and I have furnished the flat above the surgery —you'll perhaps remember them building it to house a combined practice?—and, as I wrote you, I shall work . . . for a time," she concluded, and her expression softened so that he knew she meant she would work until the family she said she longed for began to appear.

"By your standards it'll all be small, poky and shabby," she said quietly, "but by mine it'll be small, cosy and friendly; not just a house or a flat, but a home!"

Craig retreated a step and looked at her. She was as lovely as he remembered, and, by now, just as cool and self-controlled. He might have expected to have felt shattered by her reception of him, but he felt nothing, only amazement. Suddenly he realised that if Mrs. Pollard had knocked at the door, bringing the tea, neither of them had heard her and that in all probability she was standing outside, straining her ears.

He crossed to the door and opened it quickly. Mrs. Pollard, a little flustered, stood just outside the door, a tray in her hands.

"I was just about to knock," she began, but Craig took the tray from her without saying a word and moved the door shut with his foot. He was angry, more angry than he ever remembered being in his life before. Not content with making a fool of him in the eyes of Emley General *and* all their mutual friends, she had made him feel foolish in the eyes of her landlady, a woman Ellen knew he could never stand for more than a minute at a time.

"Thank you!" he said briefly just before the door closed on her curious stare. He placed the tray carefully on the table, leaving it to Ellen to pour the tea if she felt so inclined. Obviously she felt as upset as he had ever known her feel, for as her hands moved amongst the tea-things he noted her fingers were trembling.

"What do you intend to do?" he asked flatly. "What do you want *me* to do, too?"

"We're planning on a quiet wedding the first week in December," she said in a low tone. "Just a few friends. David expects he'll have a better offer from the combination by then, and that's a sort of celebration week in consequence. I've sent all the presents back to everyone who sent to . . . us," she concluded abruptly. "I should think what you ought to do is to look for some sort of reliable housekeeper. That's all you need at present!"

He was too shocked to say anything more, but one

question must be answered before he could find any peace of mind at all.

"How long have you felt like this?" he asked quietly. "Long before I went to Whemlybridge?"

"For a few years now," she said honestly, cutting across his quick "Why didn't you tell me?" with an instant "It would have spoiled what you'd planned in your work!"

"Work was something I was doing for both of us," he said with a grim quietness which sounded deadly. "You knew that. It wasn't that alone," he amended sincerely. "I *know* I can get to the top of my own particular tree . . . and I thought you wanted it that way too. *Not* to have . . . gone on would have been a betrayal of all I've worked for, studied for, believed in, a betrayal of all I firmly believe I'm really intended to do."

"I know," Ellen said, still speaking quietly. "Try not to hate me, won't you?" she managed with a brief smile.

"I don't." He realised in astonishment that that was true. Instead he felt suddenly free, free as he had not felt for years, but one thing still burned angrily in his mind.

"I . . . wish you'd told me sooner," he admitted, and was rendered almost speechless by her quick "It wouldn't have made any difference," because he knew it to be true.

"Your tea," she murmured, handing it to him and adding : "Have you booked anywhere in Emley to stay the night?"

"No." He shook his head. "I've only the one day and evening off," he explained. "I shall drive back; I'm on duty again in the morning."

"I'll make you some sandwiches," she offered, and although he felt pride should have made him refuse them, common sense told him he did not feel inclined to go into any place in Emley where almost everyone knew him, realising they would all know about Ellen and her . . . David.

He ate the dainty sandwiches quickly, accepted another cup of tea and lit cigarettes for both of them. After that he couldn't get away quickly enough. She accompanied him to the door, and subconsciously he heard the sound of Mrs. Pollard's television being turned down as they went along the hall.

"Sure you're not angry, or . . . hurt?" she asked as she leaned over the gate watching him get into the car. He shook his head. He was confused, but not as he had been when receiving her letter; that had been a bolt from the blue. Now, he reflected, scarcely realising the trend of his thoughts, he was abruptly relieved . . . and all he wanted was to discuss what had happened with someone who would really understand, someone who would put him right if he had been the one in the wrong to follow what he had believed to be his star and to allow the human side of things to take care of themselves.

"Bon voyage", he heard the words as he switched on the engine and the car began to move. It would be, he reflected as he travelled back along the road, it would be a very pleasant journey, because it was leading him back to his friend Staff Nurse Nona Hoyle!

CHAPTER 8

CRAIG hadn't realised he was thinking of Nona in terms of a refuge. He drove steadily along the road, mentally calculating it would be turned eleven o'clock by the time he reached Whemlybridge, then automatically wondering whether she would stay up to watch any of the late-night programmes or be having one of her so-called early nights. Certainly he gave no thought to the empty house which awaited his return. He wanted to talk to someone, someone upon whom he could rely to tell him whether or not he had been the supremely selfish person Ellen's words appeared to portray him, or whether the urge to become skilled in the work he loved, to develop his undoubted gift to its fullest extent, had, after all, been the right one.

"I couldn't have done anything else," he muttered to himself, waiting until the lights changed in his favour at the main entrance to the town. "Surgery's my life . . . I thought Ellen understood that! And she can say what she likes, she wouldn't have wanted a small flat of her own, maybe with the family she's carrying on about, and me living in at either Emley General or anywhere else! She'd soon have grown fed up with that kind of thing!"

The lights changed and he moved forward with the traffic. Not even thinking about it, he turned off into the road which led to the High Street and along there to where Bannister's Ryde stood. He pulled his car into a vacant space on the opposite side of the road and sat for a moment, remembering just how Ellen had looked when she told him she had been thinking along these lines for years.

98

"If only she'd had the courage to *tell* me," he reflected. "It's not like Ellen to be deceitful!"

The dreadful thought that perhaps Ellen had wanted to remain certain of his own devotion while she waited to see if she fell in love—really in love, that is—with anyone else popped into his mind, to be dismissed at once as unworthy of Ellen as he knew her.

But *did* he know her at all? The question persisted in his mind as he locked the car and pocketed the keys. He would have said so, after all these years, and events would have proved him to be completely wrong. Standing beside his car, thinking, he realised exactly how little he *did* know about his ex-fiancée. He knew she was an efficient nurse, that she liked hot, strong tea well sweetened, he knew she hated country walks, adored cats and couldn't bear dogs. In addition, he thought wryly, he now knew she wanted a home, that in some way she didn't feel quite up to the effort of becoming the wife of a consultant, at least that was how it looked to him at the moment!

"But I know much more than that about Nona!" he told himself, mentally reviewing the situation. "I know she likes cooking, reading and needlework. I know she's warm-hearted and sympathetic, not just with the patients under her care. I know she's methodical and thorough—there isn't another theatre staff nurse to touch her anywhere, I'll be bound—and I know she's thoughtful . . . she brought my watch that day without even attempting to make a personal thing of it! I know her background. All I know about Ellen's people is that she doesn't get on well with any of them, and I don't even know why."

He crossed the road and mounted the stairs to the flat the girls shared. The people opposite, he noted, had moved out, and for a second he toyed with the idea of putting Grey Walls up for immediate sale and applying for the tenancy of the vacant flat for himself.

He quelled that idea at once. He liked Grey Walls, he realised abruptly. At times he had thought it a useless extravagance, a waste of the money he had saved so painstakingly over the years so as to be able to start out with Ellen on the right foot. Now, in some curious way, he found the memory of the gracious rooms, the pleasant-looking hallway with its huge staircase rising from its well, attractive and pleasing. Even the memory of the garden, covered now with a light powdering of frosted snow, seemed wonderful when he recalled the twin windowboxes which Ellen kept on windowsills of her room with Mrs. Pollard, flowering their brief glory into the summer air for part of the year, the lifted heads of spring bulbs at other times, and most of the time, or so it seemed in memory, two plain green boxes, earth-filled.

The garden at Grey Walls might be covered in frost and some snow, but there were flourishing patches of Christmas roses under the trees, green spikes of flowering bulbs of every variety showing here and there, with their promises of beauty to come later on. No, he told himself as he rapped smartly on the door of the girls' flat, he *wouldn't* give up Grey Walls! Ellen might change her mind again . . . and even if she didn't, it was a fitting place for the man he knew himself to be and for the standing in which, he was certain, he would be held in the community before very long.

Suddenly, standing there outside the door of the flat and waiting for one of them to answer his knock, he knew he didn't particularly want Ellen to change her mind again. Right up to the moment when she had said this thought was not a new one in her mind, he had hoped to be able to persuade her to begin all over again. Yet to have planned all this, to have kept from him the knowledge that their plans for a shared future no longer appealed to her, seemed suddenly to mean he could not ever—trust her again. With that feeling all other emotion where she was concerned, seemed to die, and he felt once again as lost and lorn as he had done when he had received her letter, possibly because he had no other emotion to put in its place!

Avice wiped away the last trace of the face pack from her face, muttering under her breath. She hadn't been expecting any callers this evening, and because Nona had refused to go out, Avice had contented herself by sitting, restlessly, but none the less sitting, to watch an old film on the television and to give herself the luxury of a full-scale manicure and face-pack, one after the other!

Nona had been with her until a few minutes ago. When the film was over she had made savoury toast and coffee, then settled down to write one of her regular letters to her beloved Aunt Mary and Uncle Jack.

"I'll nip out and post this now," she had said. "I feel I'd like a breath of air, and if it's in before midnight there's a good chance they'll get it in the morning."

Avice had nodded, not speaking in case she cracked the caked pack on her face. In dumb show she had signalled she would fill their hot-water bottles, and this she had done, repeating to herself the vow she invariably made when this task fell to her lot, that sooner or later she would have to invest in an electric blanket!

She had just filled the second bottle when the knock came on the door, but before she could see who was there the pack *must* be completely removed!

"Coming!" she called as the knock was repeated. "Hang on a minute, can't you?"

She was utterly astonished to see Craig Roper standing outside. Instinctively she knew she wasn't the person he had come to see, though whenever he called he was careful to make no distinction between the two girls. She held the door open and gestured him to come inside.

"Nona's gone to the pillar-box," she explained. "I don't suppose she'll be more than a minute or so. I'll put the kettle on again."

Craig sat down in the chair he normally used, totally oblivious of the fact that between the girls it was known as 'Nona's chair,' and relaxed, it seemed, for the first time for ages. As she finished filling the kettle and turned to glance through the open door at her guest, the light from the table lamp fell on his face so attractively that, for the first time since he had come to the flat as a visitor, she thought she could see exactly what was compellingly alluring in his presence.

To this moment he had intrigued her merely as another male member of the staff of St. Jude's, an attractive member, certainly, but one of whom it was well known throughout the town and especially amongst the circle in which she lived and worked that he was engaged and shortly to be married to a girl he had been courting most of his working life.

Avice was not a poacher by nature or by inclination. She would never knowingly have tried to entice another girl's man, but there had been rumours, no end of them, that all was not well in the love life of the handsome S.S.O. To add point to the story, hadn't his first move been, on becoming established at St. Jude's, to negotiate the purchase of one of the most attractive houses in town, in one of the most expensive districts, something which, she reasoned, must have cost him at least the savings of most of his working life? In addition, he still lived in that same house . . . but alone. And tonight, she thought as she peeped at him again and saw the lines of tiredness after his double long drive, the stirrings of so many emotions, he did not in the least give the impression of a hopeful bridegroom-to-be looking eagerly forward to the date of his wedding!

"And Nona says she looks upon him as a friend in need of a friend, and that's all," she reminded herself. "She's never bothered with anyone since Trevor, so it won't mean a thing to her and it'll probably do him all the good in the world to have a light flirtation with someone who isn't going to take him seriously anyhow!"

With all her heart she wished she had not been so hasty in telling him where Nona had gone and why. She sent up a silent prayer that someone would meet her friend, someone who knew Nona well enough to keep her talking for those few minutes which Avice, fairly certain of her attractiveness to most men, was certain were all she would need.

She hurried into the living-room, cups and saucers in her hand, placing them on the table and pulling up a small stool to sit almost at his feet.

"I'm an idiot!" she began cheerfully enough. "I said Nona had gone to the pillar-box! She did, ages ago. Then she went out again. She's met a friend, a man she knows who works in the town, and went out again. I really don't know how long it'll be before she's back."

"She's gone out again?" Craig repeated as though he could not believe the evidence of his ears. "Where to?"

"How should I know?" Avice shrugged and leaned back against his knees, almost but not quite resting her red-gold head on his knee, "We don't pry into one another's affairs," she murmured.

She was almost knocked from the stool by the haste with which Craig rose to his feet. If Nona was out, then he had no intention of staying here with Avice. There was no comfort, no advice or help to be found here! He had only found one person whom he could feel he could treat as a confidant, and he was disappointed beyond all measure to learn she wasn't in, but . . . out with some other man!

"I'll be going," he muttered. "I have to get some supper out and get to bed. We shall have a full list tomorrow, I suppose." There would be no discussion now as to whether or not he had been selfish in his approach to the future of himself and Ellen! That was something he would have to work out for himself. It seemed incredible that Nona should not have mentioned another man friend, but at the same time, he reminded himself, she was an extremely attractive girl, not only in her looks but more especially in her personality! She must know most people in and around Whemlybridge, especially the more attractive male members of the staff of St. Jude's! There must be many ex-patients too, who would remember a nurse like Nona, for her selfless attitude, her thoughtful kindliness, her serene disposition.

Suddenly, almost with the force of a physical blow, it struck him just how many things about Nona would be attractive to any member of his sex. It wasn't her looks alone; pretty as she undoubtedly was Ellen's more flamboyant beauty was, in a way, far more outstanding. Yet he smiled to himself without realising the softening effect this had on his stern features, Nona's delightfully warm sympathetic personality seemed to be an open appeal to any man to take care of her, even though, as she was fond of pointing out to him and to anyone else interested, she was perfectly capable of looking after herself!

"And she is, too," he thought with reluctant admiration. "She didn't even let being jilted spoil her life! She simply set to work to remake it, and to improve her whole way of living . . . she said so herself."

Avice, seeing the softening of the stern outlines of the man's face, thought her own small ruse was succeeding. Her lip curled, ever so slightly, and he did not notice. If he *had* noticed he would never have connected the somewhat scornful expression as being anything to do with himself, but it had.

"I thought he'd be . . . different, after all Nonie's said about him," Avice told herself contemptuously. "She's put him on a pedestal. It'll be a kindness to let her know he has feet of clay, just like the rest of them!"

She had taken the softening of his expression to mean he would turn to herself for whatever comfort he had been hoping for from Nona. She was not in the least surprised. In her view most of the men she had met so far were not particularly concerned with one girl only, and her feelings one way or the other!

"I can make your supper," she said now, uncurling like a lazy kitten and looking up adoringly into his face. No one, looking at her, would have guessed how hard she was willing Nona to have met someone to talk to, someone who'd keep her out just long enough for Avice to persuade him to put his arms about her!

Craig looked at her almost as though seeing her for the first time. His mind had been so occupied by the thought that, perhaps, there was some truth in his self-applied accusations of selfishness, and he had no thought whatsoever to spare for this girl, sprawled, as he thought of it, on the floor before the fire!

This room had been a haven for him ever since the night he had opened Ellen's letter saying she was going to marry someone else. He had come here tonight, straight from Ellen's presence, looking for the same kind of down-to-earth, commonsense comfort and help he had received then, and Nona was out! And not alone, according to this girl who, he remembered guiltily, had just promised to make a meal for him!

"No," he said hastily, too hastily, Avice thought, as though he wanted to get away from her as quickly as possible. "I . . . Nona once said that Joe's was always open until midnight. I'll go back that way and get a pie or a fish supper there, thank you just the same. Tell her I called, will you, please?" he rushed on, adding and gaining the door before she had managed to get to her feet, "I can see myself out, thank you. Don't bother to come to the door."

"Well!" Avice sat back on her heels as the door closed behind him. "Evidently he hadn't come for the usual sort of comfort one might have expected!" she thought wryly, then she stood up, laughing at herself. "Serves you right," she admonished the secret Avice of whose existence she hoped no one save herself was aware! "Nona *said* theirs was a truly platonic friendship, and you just couldn't accept that, could you? You had to make up a pack of lies and hope she didn't come back too soon! I wonder what *is* keeping her? She should have been back ages ago . . . unless she *has* met some-one and stood talking."

That was, precisely, what had happened. Nona had pushed her letters into the box and had been on the point of turning away and returning to the flat, when someone tapped her on the arm.

"Excuse me," the young man began diffidently, "it *is* Nurse Hoyle, isn't it? It's difficult to recognise you in this light and without your cloak or uniform coat!"

It was equally difficult, Nona reflected, responding to his greeting, to recognise the young man himself. He looked so very different in a sports jacket under a huge, enveloping car-coat, a soft hat at a rakish angle on his head, the head she had previously only seen on top of a pair of fairly narrow shoulders as he had attended to her modest needs at the corner bank.

"Mr. Horncastle?" she queried, and felt a silly sense of relief when he nodded.

"I'm sorry if I startled you," he apologised, "but I felt I *must* try and have a word with you. You and your friend share a flat in Bannister's Ryde, don't you?"

"There's one to let," he informed her eagerly as she nodded. "I've tried to find out where to apply, but no one seems to know, and we have to get out . . . my wife and I, that is. No children allowed, you see, and she's expecting a baby before long. We've tried all over the place, but someone told me if an existing tenant would vouch for us, we'd have an excellent chance of getting it. Is that true?"

"I can't say, Mr. Horncastle, not truthfully, but I do know the owner, and she's very nice and friendly. I'm sure she doesn't object to children, either! In fact I know she doesn't, there are two in the flat above us. And a dog! I could give you her address and I can phone and tell her what nice people you are," she laughed lightly. "I can vouch for that! You managed things beautifully for me when I badly needed that overdraft for my holiday last year, and you scarcely knew me then! Would that be any help, do you think?"

"I think it may well be, thank you," he said gratefully. "As for the overdraft, that was business, and I was only too pleased to be able to arrange matters to help you over a sticky patch. This is a more personal thing . . . and I really *am* anxious, because of Doreen, you know. She's nervous enough already, without all this worry about whether or not we'll have a roof over our heads by the time the baby does arrive!"

"When you get into the flat I'll come and have a talk with her, Mr. Horncastle," Nona promised confidently. "I'll see Miss Spofforth personally. She's the lady who owns the place. It was left to her by her father and she turned the whole house into flats and went to live in a little cottage just out of town, all by herself except for the elderly housekeeper who's been in the family for years! I'll see what I can do," she promised, and, almost overwhelming her with thanks, the young man fell into step beside her and began to walk the short distance back to Bannister's Ryde.

Across the road Craig stood beside his car. The sensible thing, he realised, would have been to get in and drive off immediately to Joe's, the open-air mobile hot food van which stood at the other end of the market place every night of the week save Sunday. Curiosity had impelled him to stand there for a few moments, although if, as Avice had said, Nona had gone out with some man or other it was extremely unlikely she would be coming in just now.

He stiffened as he caught sight of her unmistakable form advancing along the pavement on the opposite side of the road. Avice had been right, he reflected. She *was* with a man, a young man who, to Craig's almost certain knowledge, was not a member of the staff of St. Jude's. That meant only one thing. Either he was one of the many ex-patients who must have cause to remember Nona appreciatively, or he was someone she had met—perhaps at a dance, perhaps at the cinema or through some activity of which he knew nothing—but wherever she had met him or how long she had known him, they were evidently on friendly terms, for they were laughing and talking together like old friends as they walked along.

He didn't stop to analyse why, but abruptly he knew he could not bear to watch a moment longer. Soon she would be opposite to the point where his car was parked, and although he was shaded by the leafless branches of the old elm which towered above him, he felt somehow she would know he was there, watching her.

He jumped into his car and slammed the door shut, switching on the engine and driving off in the direction of Joe's almost before he had realised what he was going to do. Joe was putting up his shutters for the night, but he recognised Craig as he got out of the car and greeted him with a cheerful smile.

"Understand you've had a day off, Doc," he grinned. "Not before time, if you ask me! What's it to be, then? And are you going to stop and eat here as I'm packin' up, or take it with you, all nice and hot?"

"I'll take it with me, Joe," Craig said hastily, anxious only to prevent the man talking further. "I don't much care what it is, either, providing it's hot! I expect I'll have a busy day tomorrow, so I want to get to bed as quickly as possible tonight."

"They do let you get some rest, then, some nights?" Joe enquired chattily as he wrapped up a selection of choice pieces he thought Craig might enjoy. "With you living away from the hospital, like, it'll come in handy against not hearing them night calls I've read so much about."

"Nearly always," Craig admitted, smiling as he wondered just where and what exactly Joe *had* read. "If there's an emergency, of course, I'm called out, but so far, touch wood, there have only been three which have required my help when I'm supposed to be sleeping! Of course," he added mainly to himself as Joe couldn't be expected to understand what he was talking about, "there's the R.S.O. always on call, and if it's anything to do with Sir Alex's patients then he has to be informed as well."

"And they wait till morning, unless it's really bad, I know," Joe nodded knowledgeably, and Craig didn't argue. There wasn't anything he could say to convince Joe that whatever he had read wasn't the absolute and accurate truth.

"That'll be five and fourpence, Doc," Joe pocketed the money and closed his shutters. "Have a good night," he called after Craig. "And enjoy it while it's hot!"

Craig drove slowly back to Grey Walls. He could not imagine himself enjoying anything particularly that night! He put the car in the roomy garage and looked round the four walls, remembering how he had imagined he would have room here for a small runabout which Ellen would be able to use for herself, but somehow, now, he could only picture Nona calmly parking a small car of some sort, some Mini or other, alongside his more opulent Rover.

"I've got that girl on my brain!" he told himself, slamming the roll-up door closed and retreating into the house. "If only I'd been able to *talk* to her!" he thought, then a mental picture came into his mind of Nona already 'talking,' talking with a strange man as they walked side by side along the road, laughing together.

He had warmed the tea-pot as she had instructed him

he should do, and was just in the act of spooning the tea into the pot when he could almost hear her voice beside him saying "and one for the pot!" as she invariably did when she made the tea.

He sat down abruptly, his purchased supper still in the wrappings on the hotplate, the kettle bubbling and boiling unheeded. It was uncanny, so uncanny he looked round wondering if he were the victim of hallucination, but there was nothing and no one to disturb him. The graceful grandmother clock he had bought because he had liked the beautiful mahogany case showed it to be well past the witching hour, but he felt bewitched!

Abruptly he realised why he had not been upset when Ellen had moved out of his reach, when she had stood with the table between them, as though, he thought contemptuously, he was likely to try and take her by force!

He hadn't really wanted her to ask for her ring again! He hadn't wanted her to say she would forget David Dearby and all the plans they had made together! If she had said that, he reflected, he would have had to accept it, but it was a merciful thing that Ellen had been adamant!

He had wanted, he knew now, the sure comfort of Nona's common sense, Nona's smile and Nona's companionship. It was to her he had turned instinctively, and just as instinctively he had been certain she would not let him down! When he had discovered she was out —and seen for himself, not many minutes later—that she was out with an unknown man—he had felt, he realised now, far more shocked than when he had first read Ellen's letter breaking their engagement. Then he had been hurt—or, more correctly, his pride had been hurt —because everyone knew they were to be married, that he had bought Grey Walls for her, and that for weeks he had been planning for their future together.

No one but himself, he thought now, knew of what he

felt for Nona Hoyle. He hadn't known himself until this minute, but he knew now, and beyond all shadow of doubt, beyond, even, all reason, because they had only known one another as friends, that this girl was the love of his life, the one person who would mean more to him than life itself, and would do so until he died.

CHAPTER 9

WHEN Craig started his car Nona looked across the street. It was dark, and she could not see the registration number of the vehicle, but the shape of the man behind the wheel looked very familiar, and, if the driver wasn't Craig and the car wasn't his, why in the world was a car like that parked almost opposite the flat?

"You will do what you can for us, won't you, Nurse?" Phil Horncastle was asking pleadingly. "I know people have babies with every normality possible, even though at times it may not be all the bed of roses it's cracked up to be!" he smiled. "Perhaps it's just because there's been this to-do about our having to get out of the flat we've been in ever since we were married, I just don't know. Whatever the reason, Doreen's far from well and just lately she's been making a very big thing of this coming birth! She *will* be all right, won't she, Nurse?" he queried anxiously.

"Of course." Nona's smile, as always, was very reassuring. "I'd have to see her, of course, before I can make any comment really, but I take it she is under the doctor, seeing him regularly and all that sort of thing?"

"Oh, yes. We have Dr. Prescomb, you know. She goes to the ante-natal clinics and all that sort of thing. I'm not really in favour of her doing that, either!" he went on in some concern. "She meets so many people who are full of . . . what do you call 'em? Old wives' tales, they tell her things that scare her half to death, the silly things."

"Your wife ought not to listen to them, either!" Nona said quietly. "I know some of these people are a positive menace, and there isn't a thing one can do about them except put on a cheerful smile and tell them—as I'm sure will be true—the doctor is pleased and so is the midwife . . . you *have* engaged one, I take it?"

"Nurse Plowlett's our district midwife," Phil said promptly. "*She* says Doreen's fine . . . if she wouldn't worry so much! I'm sure once we get into a flat where she knows they won't mind her having a baby, she'll get over all this nervous tension. I'm sure that's all it is."

"I should imagine so," Nona agreed, nodding. "I'll do what I can," she promised a second—or was it a third time?—but he hadn't quite finished.

She listened, knowing it helped him to talk, and understanding more than he realised why his wife was strung up and upset. She had taken her midwifery, thank goodness, and she was well able to reassure him that in the event of their getting the vacant flat opposite to her own, she would most willingly pop in and attend to Doreen should the baby arrive unexpectedly or during the night, or at any rate that she would stay, if she were at home, until Nurse Plowlett or the doctor or both arrived.

She escaped at last and was speeding upstairs when she met the young woman from the flat above her own, the mother of the two children she had mentioned to Phil Horncastle. The girl—she was little more—was on her way to Nona's flat to ask if she might use the telephone. By her description of the symptoms of the child who was sick, Nona felt fairly certain this was nothing more than a mild bilious attack and that it would be unfair to have the doctor come out at this late hour when, in all probability, he had not long since finished his work for the day!

Nona, being Nona, accompanied the young woman back to her own flat, saw the baby now sleeping soundly and overwhelmingly grateful that Nona had spared her the unnecessary summoning of the doctor, "For he says I'm one of his 'fretful mums,' as he calls us, Nurse Hoyle," she smiled. "I don't suppose any man can know what it's really like, being a mum, I mean. I know they can't know . . . oh, I'm getting all confused, but you *do* understand what I mean, don't you? I get so worried if either of them are just a little bit off colour."

Her husband was a night worker on the new, huge telephone exchange just outside Whemlybridge, and Nona could well understand her anxiety, whether mis-placed or not, when anything appeared to be wrong with either of the two children left in her care. For the same reason she could understand why Peggy wanted a dog, not just as company, but because she hated being alone so many nights in the week, "And I can't keep running up and down and bothering other people, especially after I've got the children to bed."

Nona assured her it had been a pleasure to be of some small assistance, fussed the dog, a huge shaggy creature with pleading brown eyes and a plumy tail, refused an offer of a cup of tea by saying Avice would have supper waiting, and finally ran downstairs to her own flat.

Avice was ready for bed. She was listening to the record player, a stack of Elvis Presley records pandering to her fondness for that singer. She switched the instru-ment off as Nona came in.

"Your boy-friend's been for you," she said casually. "Left a while ago. Where on earth have you been? Delivering your letter by hand or something?"

"Got talking," Nona said, "I'll tell you about it later. What time did he go? You *do* mean Craig Roper, don't you? And incidentally, how many times must I tell you he's *not* my boy-friend?"

"He's been gone almost three-quarters of an hour, I should say," Avice yawned. "Boy-friend or not," she said slyly, "he didn't want anything to do with me! Once he found out you weren't here he was off like the shot from a gun! He didn't seem any too happy," she added thoughtfully, "not as you'd expect a man to behave when he's just been reunited with his ex-fiancée."

"Is he?" Nona asked quickly. "I mean . . . are they engaged again?"

"He didn't say," Avice admitted. "In fact he said scarcely anything at all, mainly that he was going to pick something to eat up at Joe's and go to bed because he expected there'd be a busy day ahead of you both tomorrow. I should think," she added, glancing at the clock, "he'll have eaten whatever he managed to buy at that time of night and gone to bed. He looked very tired, so that's what he'll have done if he's at all wise!"

"Couldn't you have made him some coffee or something?" Nona asked a little tartly. She would never have believed she could be so disappointed by missing seeing him like this!

"I offered to make supper for him," Avice said sulkily, remembering only too clearly that Craig Roper was one of the few men who had rebuffed her, no matter how politely he had done it the fact remained that was precisely what he *had* done! "I've told you I offered to make his supper, and he muttered about eating and going to bed, then he just went."

Nona did not want to press the matter further at this point, but this behaviour was so unlike that of the Craig she knew she just could not believe it possible. There must have been some mistake, just as he must have something he wanted to tell her, to talk over with her or he wouldn't have come straight to the flat on his return to Whemlybridge. She hesitated a moment, then made up her mind.

"I'll telephone him," she said decisively. "If he was as upset as you appear to think he was, then he won't be asleep as yet! If he wants to talk about something, maybe it'll help if he gets it over with and then he'll perhaps rest better!"

"What a lot of concern about someone who's nothing to you except the man you work with!" Avice scoffed. "Shall I make another cuppa and anything to eat?" she asked resignedly. "If our strong, silent man's really prepared to talk then there's no knowing how long he'll take about doing it! Depends on what he wants to talk about, I suppose! Anyhow, you won't want me eavesdropping, so I'll make a snack and if you're not through with your conversation by that time I'll take mine to bed. O.K.?"

"O.K.," Nona said, looking up Craig's number and wondering at the same time if she really ought to telephone him. It was one thing to chat with him in off-duty time, simply because he sought her out and seemed nowadays to depend more or less on her understanding and her company, and quite another to telephone him at his home, and at an hour when most normal people would be thinking of their sleep!

"He must have wanted to see me, anyway!" she reasoned to herself. "He said he'd come here straight away . . . no, those had not been his words. 'If things don't go the way I . . . want them to,' he had said, 'you will still be the same, won't you, Nona?'" and, like a perfect idiot and as though she hadn't already learned her lesson, she had assured him that she *would* still be the same.

"The same idiot who lets herself get involved with other people's affairs, lets them trample on her, use her and make a fool of her over and over again!" she told herself, sitting back on her heels to think out just what she could say to Craig when he answered the telephone. She hoped he would not have just dropped off to sleep and would resent her telephoning at this hour of the night! If only she hadn't gone out to the post-box just when she had done! If only she hadn't met Philip Horncastle and stood talking for such a long time . . . but she had known she was helping him, and, through him, his nervously inclined young wife and mother-to-be!

After that, her thoughts ran on, if only she hadn't encountered Peggy on the stairway! The entire evening, since the moment she had gone to the pillar-box, seemed to have been spent in trying to help, advise, console someone or other with whom she came into contact! Now, she sighed without knowing quite why, if it were not too late and if she could awaken him, she would do her best to help Craig in whatever dilemma faced him at this moment.

She could not possibly have imagined the exact dilemma which did indeed face Craig just then. When he came face to face with the real reason why he wanted to see Nona, to talk to her, no one could have been more shocked and surprised than Craig himself. All the time, ever since she had first taken him to the flat, he had believed sincerely he was thinking of her only as he might have thought of a beloved sister or a very close friend. The knowledge that, in fact, he *loved* her had come just when he had seen her out with another man, and, apparently, on very friendly terms.

"I can't mess her life up as, apparently, I've messed up Ellen's," he thought miserably. "I think Ellen and I must have come together mainly because we were both a little lonely, both scared of committing ourselves to any sort of a future together! We ought to have known, both of us! If one isn't prepared to take a risk because one is in love, then one really can't be in love at all! Ellen says she always wanted a home, children and someone to come home to her! Yet she never *said* so. I know she says she kept quiet because I was so set on getting to the top of my profession! I'm on my way . . . but would I have wanted a girl I loved to live in a flat on her own, hiding the fact she was my wife in case Matron asked her to leave her job? Would I have wanted her to take the risk of a family, of having to put up with all the awkward hours I've put up with all these years, with all the petty schemes to save enough to get a good start when the time was right?"

The answer was simple. With the right girl, he reflected, it would have been a kind of adventure! With

Nona, laughing together at difficulties, striving together and sharing the joy each time a new object was surmounted, there would have been something more than wonderful in the doing, there would have been the thrill of mutual achievement, the sense of accomplishment . . . together!

That, he decided, was what he had loved most, without knowing it, from the very beginning where Nona was concerned. It was something which he had never experienced at all with Ellen. She had enjoyed her own moments of glory as she was promoted up her own ladder of success, but even when she was given her Ward Sistership, he remembered, he had been on duty the same night and they had been unable to go out together to celebrate! When he was free to do so, about four evenings later, she had been as cool and as composed as ever and said it didn't matter, that it was childish to make anything of something as inevitable as this had been!

It wasn't really inevitable! He remembered his own arguments so clearly. Many girls made their S.R.N., went on to be staff nurses and, in many cases, remained in that state for a longer time than Ellen had done. Many too, he reflected now, married at this stage of their careers or went into welfare work or something else . . . and in his opinion her Ward Sistership had really been something they might well have made into an occasion.

Altogether, looking back on the years which had gone by since he had first met Ellen and admired her pale, cold, proud-looking beauty, theirs had been more like a business partnership than a love affair.

"It hasn't really been a love affair at all," he thought now, "not in any sense of the word! No wonder she's looked for someone else! I only hope she isn't going to make the same mistake all over again! That's her business, though. Nona's mine."

Yet she wasn't his business, he reminded himself. She

was a pretty, sweet-natured girl who'd gone out of her way to be helpful and kind at a time when he was—or believed he was—in the throes of despair.

"And all the time it was my pride which was hurt!" he marvelled at himself. "Good thing I didn't attempt to go in for my psychology degree! I can't even analyse myself and find out what's wrong with my own affairs, much less even try to help anyone else! Nona has a much better idea of how to sort out people's problems—emotional problems, that is—than I have!"

There it was again! Somehow or other every thought seemed to lead right back to her, whether he liked it or not! It was as though, in some inexplicable way, she was part of his life, part of his heart and mind now and for all time in a way such as had never happened where Ellen was concerned. Ellen, he knew, he could see one weekend and not worry in the least if he neither saw or heard from her for the next two weeks! Where Nona was concerned, he wanted to know *all* about her, where she was, with whom she had been and why!

"And none of it is any of my business!" he reflected gloomily. "It wouldn't be fair for me to say anything to her now . . . not about how I've realised I feel about her! She'd think it was a sort of on-the-rebound thing, and it isn't! There wasn't anything to rebound off from, I know that now, but no girl would ever believe me! Nona least of all, because she saw how stupidly upset I was . . . and even though she may realise that was hurt pride, wounded vanity, call it what you like—it was real enough, she wouldn't, I'm sure, like to think I'd turned to her just as a substitute, and whichever way I look at it I know that's how it's going to seem to her!"

The smell of charred paper recalled him to the present and he looked across to where the supper he had purchased was turning a dingy brown on the top of the hotplate. That, he reflected, was just the paper, and although he couldn't feel the charred paper scent would have been very good for the parcel it contained, he knew he would have to eat something or go hungry to St. Jude's in the morning, because once he managed to get to sleep tonight he realised it would take a very real effort to get him out of bed and on the way to the hospital in the morning!

The kettle had boiled almost dry and switched itself off with the safety device. He rose, feeling suddenly stiff, old and very tired. Common sense told him this was weariness, the double long drive following the hard weeks in the theatre with little or no relaxation. Something other than common sense told him more truthfully that had he felt Nona was as free as he had believed her to be, free for him to attempt to win her love for himself, his weariness would be forgotten.

"She isn't and I can't," he told himself firmly as he refilled the kettle and warmed the tea-pot all over again. "It wouldn't be fair! Had she been a person like Ellen, cool and self-contained, thinking more of her own affairs than those of anyone else, I could have done it. Nona's all . . . give. If she thought I was interested in her she'd say the man meant nothing, that no man had meant anything to her since the time she was jilted! *He* must have been a fool! Wherever he goes, whatever girl he meets and has married, he'll never find anyone so un-self-seeking as Nona Hoyle! I'm glad he *did* go, though. I'll not intrude," he promised himself, scraping the over-heated remnants of his supper on to a plate. "I'll wait and watch. It shouldn't be too difficult to find out whether or not this man means anything to her. In the meantime she *must* feel free, free to please herself, to find her happiness—and her love—wherever she feels she can! If she doesn't feel free of me, of any obligation to help me sort out my own emotional tangles, she'll be silly enough to let her own life go hang and try and patch up mine! I can't be cad enough to take that sort of mean advantage!"

He had just made this decision, a decision he told himself he must adhere to no matter at what cost to himself, when the phone in the hall shrilled through the silence. For a long minute or so he let it continue to ring. It *could* be someone at St. Jude's. There *could* be an emergency and he might be needed. Or it *could* equally well be Nona, returned from wherever she had been with her unknown friend, phoning because Avice had told her he'd called.

"If it's her," he promised himself, going to the instrument on suddenly reluctant feet, "I must remember . . . not to even appear to need either sympathy or help! I've got to let her think . . . what she likes." He knew he couldn't hope to let her think he and Ellen had patched up their broken engagement. If she thought that, then, along with everyone else in St. Jude's—and for all he knew probably half of Whemlybridge as well—would be expecting the wedding plans to be made more or less immediately, and Ellen to come along to reside somewhere in the town. Or, since everyone would presume the wedding would be in Emley, for him; to be making plans for a decent period of vacation to utilise as a honeymoon, and for the decorators and furnishers to move into Grey Walls almost at once.

He picked up the telephone and waited a moment. St. Jude's night operator would have spoken at once, so that he knew before she spoke who was calling.

"Hello?" he said curtly, almost, he thought, as though he had been dragged from sleep and was resentful. If that was the impression he gave, well and good. It would be as good and as reasonable excuse for his apparent short temper as anything he might think up on the spur of the moment.

"Craig Roper here," he continued briefly. "Who's calling?"

"It's Nona, Craig." His heart seemed to contract as he heard the small, slightly scared sound her voice made over the wires. Nona wasn't the type to be easily upset. Perhaps his tone had put her off whatever she had intended to say, and, in the circumstances, perhaps that was as well!

"What do you want?" he demanded, hating himself but knowing he was doing it to protect her happiness. Her happiness with someone else, he reminded himself bitterly, with the unknown man to whom he had seen her talking when she had believed him still with Ellen.

"Avice said you'd called here," she said quietly. "I'd only just popped out to the pillar-box. . . ."

"So she said." He cut her short, he didn't want her to have to lie and he couldn't bring himself to tell her Avice had said she'd been to the pillar-box and gone out again. "Have you just come in?" he heard the tone of his voice and mentally shuddered. What must she be thinking of him?

"I. . . ." Nona hesitated. What she had to say sounded silly; that she had been up to the flat above, that she had spent most of the evening reassuring a man she scarcely knew that she would do her best to find accommodation for himself, his wife and an unborn child where they could be reasonably sure of being welcome and helped if necessary? That she had spent what was left of the time before she had finally come into her own flat to go to bed, helping a young frightened mother and being instrumental in preventing one local doctor from one unnecessary night call?

"I've been in a little while," she managed at last, puzzled by the tone of his voice, the words he was using. There was nothing wrong in either tone or words, but there was nothing friendly either!

"Then I suggest you go to bed as quickly as possible," Craig said coldly, "and get a good night's sleep—as I was trying to do," he ended with what seemed, to Nona, angry politeness. "Goodnight."

"Goodnight," Nona echoed in such a small forlorn

voice that he felt compelled to add, even though it was against his better judgement, "If you wanted to know how things have gone, I can tell you they have sorted themselves out quite satisfactorily. Goodnight," and before she could comment he had replaced the receiver, feeling an utterly objectionable person as he padded back to the kitchen where, in self-disgust, he flung the outraged remains of his supper into the boiler furnace and retired to bed.

CHAPTER 10

CRAIG'S mood of self-disgust lasted until he fell asleep and was with him when he awakened in the morning. As he shaved he could hear in imagination, the forlorn tones of Nona as she had said goodnight. She had sounded, he felt, like a child who had run to someone, anxious to be friendly, only to be unexpectedly rebuffed, and was hurt in consequence.

"It's for her own good," he muttered, glaring at his reflection. "If she knew Ellen was still determined to marry her precious David, she'd be worrying about me . . . and how can I tell her why I'm *glad* Ellen's found David when Nona's obviously found someone, after all, who can take the place of whatever his name was who let her down some time ago?"

He went off to St. Jude's in an angry frame of mind. Mrs. Lom, arriving as usual as he was on the point of leaving, looked after him anxiously, her brow furrowed.

"Time enough to look like that when he's married to that woman, whoever she is!" she observed to the vacuum cleaner as she pulled it out from its hiding place under the stairs. "Why he wants to bother with a body like that . . . Whemlybridge ain't good enough for her, I suppose, when there's a sweet little body like Nurse Hoyle close to hand, I'm hanged if I know! Stands to reason there must be something queer behind her never even coming to see what the place looks like! No wonder he looks like the bad end of a thunderstorm when he goes off to the hospital of a mornin'. I could tell 'im something about women like that," she muttered darkly, adding to herself with a disconsolate sniff, "but he wouldn't deign to listen, not him!" and she began her work with a feeling of high satisfaction because at last, even if only when speaking to herself, she had been able to use one of the big words Sister Jarvis used in everyday conversation.

It wasn't only in his own home or on his way to the hospital that a change was noticeable in the new S.S.O. Mike, the cheery main doors porter, noticed the stern, unrelenting expression, the firm set to the mouth and the purposeful way in which Craig strode into St. Jude's that morning. Exactly like Mrs. Lom he placed the blame for this squarely on the shoulders of the unknown woman everyone had heard he was going to marry.

"Must be a hoity-toity piece," he observed to Sam, his fellow-porter on the main doors. "Can't think how it is a nice bloke like Mr. Roper can get himself taken in by a girl like that! She's a Sister in Emley General, somebody said. All I can say is, if she can't make up her mind to fall in with what the man's doing, then she's the wrong sort of girl to be a wife to somebody like His Nibs. He'll go a long way, you mark my words! By the time Sir Alex's finally made up his mind to retire, there'll be someone there more than ready and able to step into his shoes. But he'll need the right wife!"

"Aye," Sam said laconically, pushing an empty trolley before him and casting an appreciative eye on two junior nurses as they swished past, their uniforms crisp as the morning. "Where'll he find 'er?" he asked of no one in particular, adding, "the right wife, I mean. They don't come in Christmas stockings, you know!"

"Don't mention Christmas stockings to me just now!" Mike responded with a mock shudder. "Sister Lewis was asking only yesterday if I'd help sort through that mound of toys and things we've been sent. Result of some sort of appeal from some actress on television, you know. No," he finally decided to answer Sam's comment, "they don't come in Christmas stockings, but there's one or two girls in and around St. Jude's wouldn't make him a bad parner! I'd thought him and Staff Theatre. . . ."

"No . . . o," Sam scratched his head and looked forbidding. He was one of the most fervent gossips of the entire hospital and prided himself on knowing more about everyone than most of them knew about themselves. "Staff Hoyle," he said reflectively, "is one of the few women a man'd be able to trust. Trouble was, *she* trusted the wrong man! He let 'er down, and I don't think she'll be in all that much of a hurry to take up with anybody else! I thought at one time. . . ."

He let his remarks trail off into silence, and then, seeing the brisk form of Sister Jarvis approaching at the far end of the corridor he broke into a loud-voiced discussion as to how many patients required the use of an ambulance that morning.

In the theatre it was much the same thing. The R.S.O. felt he had encountered a total stranger, so clipped and short were Craig's words to him that morning. The anaesthetist fumbled as he set up his complicated machine, and Sister shot a reproachful glance in Craig's direction as much as to say there really had been no necessity to speak so sharply to his colleague!

Even Nona came in for a sharp reprimand which was as hurtful as it was totally unexpected, but she bit back any expression of hurt or dismay, forcing herself to say quietly "Certainly, sir," in the most ordinary tone she could summon. All the same, the hurt showed in her eyes, and Craig, miserably aware of the fact, went through his work with a mechanical precision which was so unlike him that he knew she was wondering what could be wrong.

He hurried from the theatre as quickly as possible, once the operations for the day were concluded. He was in his car and out of the staff car park before the theatre was cleared, which was, to say the least of it, most unusual for him.

Nona completed her work, made certain everything in

the theatre, the recovery room and anaesthetic room was in order, then she walked quietly and swiftly to the staff sitting-room for a coffee. Somehow she did not want to go back to the flat just yet, and Avice, she knew, would be an hour or so before she was free since she was working a split shift that day.

"What's wrong with the S.S.O. today?" Staff Vernon asked casually as Nona drew herself a coffee from the automatic machine in the corner. "I met him in the corridor and it was as much as he could do to pass the time of day! That's not like him!" she said firmly, and Nona remembered Madge Vernon had been one of Craig's most fervent admirers from the first day of his appointment to St. Jude's.

"I don't know," she answered with careful truth. "Perhaps he isn't feeling too well. The weather. . . ."

"Weather my foot!" Madge said inelegantly. "He went off for the day to see that fiancée of his, you know that, don't you?" she looked directly at Nona as she added: "Of course you do! You have to know, you've been such a friend of his since he first came here, more or less. At least you're the only person on the staff apart from Anderson and his wife I've heard of that he's ever been seen out with, and someone told me they'd seen you both at the Falcon one evening." Her eyes dared Nona to deny this, and she answered as quietly as she could, determined as ever to avoid any gossip either about Craig or about herself and her own affairs.

"We went one evening," she confirmed, "but we'd been working late and there wasn't anywhere else open. I don't suppose he felt like going back to his house and cooking."

"What's wrong with the canteen here?" Madge demanded, answering her own question: "I suppose he didn't want to . . . mix as much as all that, not if he's expecting his fiancée to join him before long. Is she coming, do you know, Hoyle?"

"As I understand it, she is," Nona said evenly, hoping

the betraying colour wouldn't fly into her cheeks. She didn't want to have to answer Madge's questions any further, otherwise it was more than likely she would find herself giving away the fact that Craig had come to the flat on the same night he had visited Ellen, and there would have been more gossip, perhaps not all of it kindly.

"When?" Madge shot the question at her, eyeing her closely, but Nona was prepared for that.

"I really don't know any more about it than anyone else," she said quietly. "After all, it *is* his business . . . and hers! I'm sure he'll let us all know when the wedding's to take place!" and with that final remark she pitched her cardboard beaker into the waste basket and prepared to leave the sitting-room.

"Sorry," Madge said lightly, watching her. "Didn't know you were touchy about him and his affairs! I thought you were immune from the gossip which intrigues the rest of us!"

Nona left the remark unanswered save for a slight smile as she walked out, but her heart was aching as she reflected that she too had thought she knew more about Craig Roper than the rest of them! She had believed she was helping him, had, indeed, really helped him, and that he was her friend. This new attitude on his part was most hurtful, and the fact that she could think of no real reason for it was the most hurtful part of all.

Walking down to the bus stop she suddenly halted, struck by such an impossible thought that she was almost laughing. Almost, but not quite! What if Craig's attitude had anything to do with the fact that she had not been at home when he called? He would have expected her to be either waiting, because she had said she would 'always be the same' however matters had gone for him in Emley. If she wasn't in the living-room, something tasty on the stove, he would have imagined her to have already gone to bed with instructions left with Avice to call her if she should come.

He *had* called, and she had not been at home. She hadn't even telephoned him until much later! He might well have been wondering where she could be at that time of night!

Common sense, as she thought of it later, took over as the bus lumbered to a halt. There was absolutely no tangible reason why he should have wished to see her! When she had spoken to him over the telephone, almost as an afterthought to their brief conversation he had said, "If you wanted to know how things have gone I can tell you they've sorted themselves out quite satisfactorily," or words to that effect.

She went upstairs on the bus, something she did not often do because it seemed such an effort for so short a journey, but there was no smoking on the downstairs floor, and somehow she felt the deep and urgent need of a cigarette. She had to lean across the seat and ask the woman in front if she would give her a light from the match she had just struck to light her own cigarette. Smoking so seldom, she carried neither lighter nor matches.

She drew deeply on the small white tube. Although the smoke made her cough a little at first, before she had reached the end of her cigarette she was convinced she felt much calmer than before.

"We're just friends," she told herself firmly. "If a friend can't choose when he's to call or not, when to be friendly at work or not, then it seems I'm the one lacking in understanding him! I said I would always be the same . . . and here I am, feeling badly done to because his manner's so different, not only with me, but with everyone. Perhaps his fiancée's made some conditions he's going to find it hard to adhere to . . . though what they could be I can't possibly imagine!"

She knew, deep in her heart, the truth was that she

was secretly afraid as to the possible reason for Craig's changed manner. Had he changed only towards herself, she would have thought he was regretting the fact that she had been the one person to see his disturbance when Ellen had written, ending their engagement. That, she felt, she would have understood only too well. He would shut the memory out of his own mind, but he would never be certain, whatever she might say, that she could succeed in shutting it out of hers!

The fact that he had changed in manner towards everyone, even the theatre porter with whom he had always exchanged a joke on his arrival, seemed more than significant. Whichever way she looked at it, it seemed to her disturbed imagination that it definitely pointed to some further upset, some further quarrel with the girl he was hoping to marry.

"Whatever did happen," she assured herself as she fitted her key in the lock and went into the flat, "I somehow feel fairly certain he had a miserable visit, whether the end result was as satisfactory as he claims it to have been or not!"

No one, least of all Craig Roper himself, could guess how deeply worried and disturbed she was about his well being. He too was feeling acutely miserable, as he too walked into his empty house, shuddering a little despite the warmth of his central heating. Somehow, since he had come to know Nona so much better, the emptiness of his lonely house hurt him more than he would have believed possible.

He turned up the thermostat almost automatically, took the pre-cooked, frozen packaged "dinner for one" from his pocket and put it to heat up, thinking how much better it would have been if he had bought something in the shop which Nona, with her clever fingers and born cook's imagination, could have turned into a tasty dish.

"Stop that!" he admonished himself sternly. "Nona

shops once a week or twice at the outside estimate. She plans her meals ahead. She wouldn't thank you or anyone else for disrupting her scheme and diet plan for both of them!"

Nona! Even her name was like something out of a song, or a poem, he thought. Ellen was as cool and as remote as the girl herself. Somehow, no matter how hard he tried he had never been able to work up any romantic notions where her name was concerned, even her second name, Mona, seemed cool, aloof and remote!

"Nona," he said it over and over again to himself, feeling foolish, but enjoying the sound of her name on his tongue just the same. "Nona Hoyle. Nona Roper. . . ."

Briskly he took himself to task, dismising these foolish ideas. She wouldn't be Nona Hoyle much longer, it would appear, and he didn't even know the name of the man he'd seen with her the night he'd been to Emley!

He picked up the afternoon's post which Mrs. Lom had left, as usual, on the hall table. The top of the pile was a letter in handwriting he recognised immediately, but this time he was in no hurry to open the envelope and find out what Ellen had to say. He stood for a moment, mentally contrasting the two girls. It wasn't very easy to summon up a mental image of Ellen, he discovered, and for a moment wondered why it should be so difficult when, not so long ago, he had only to close his eyes to see the colour of her hair, the way it was always severely held back whether she was wearing her uniform cap or not, and the proud carriage of her head, her straight, always supremely erect spine, the shoulders squared as though she were mentally bracing herself against all odds.

It was a very different matter to think of Nona. He had no need to close his eyes, even, and he could imagine her standing there in front of him, her hair shining as it swung about her face the way it did when she wasn't on duty.

There was a vast difference between the two girls, he reflected, more than a difference in physical appearance, it was something in the very physical nature of the girls themselves. Ellen, he reflected, had never made him feel in the least bit necessary. She had her own career, and, until they had talked the other night, seemed perfectly satisfied with it and with the way her future was shaping in her chosen profession. Even in her arrangements with David Dearby, he remembered, she had been careful to arrange her own job to suit herself and her own requirements.

Nona was a different person altogether. Perfectly capable in her job, every bit as capable a nurse as was Ellen, yet warm and friendly where both staff and patients—and the relatives of patients, he thought, smiling—were concerned. When he and Ellen had gone out together he had invariably had the feeling she didn't much mind whether he was there or not. She would watch everyone else in the restaurant or theatre or in the cinema, and he always felt—although she never said anything to give him occasion for such thoughts, simply, he felt 'looked' it—she was mentally comparing him, and not to his advantage, with every other man in sight. She would look intently at the small box of chocolates which she insisted was enough to buy on an evening out, and then sigh in an exaggerated manner if someone else in the same row at the theatre or the cinema had a larger and more expensive box bought for them.

Nona wouldn't behave like that, he was certain. They had never yet been out together on any entertainment excursion, as he thought of it, but when they had gone to the Falcon, when they had enjoyed an occasional snack at Joe's or shared a meal in the flat, she had given him her undivided attention without intruding upon his inner self.

"She makes me feel," he reflected, "as though she *depends* on my company whenever we're together.

She seems to suggest that without my being present she wouldn't be enjoying herself at all. It's all imagination, I suppose, but she never so much as looks bored for a second, she didn't seem bored even on that dreadful evening when I fell asleep in her chair. Just smiled and said she thought Avice was coming in . . . as though I hadn't guessed that for myself, all the row that girl made coming upstairs!"

He slit the flap of the envelope thoughtfully. Whatever Ellen had to say he might as well read it and get it over with! He wondered vaguely if she had been thoughtless enough as to send him an invitation to her forthcoming wedding, but when he withdrew the single sheet of notepaper he saw for himself it was an ordinary letter.

As always, the letter itself was brief and to the point. When they had first corresponded he had teased her about her 'businesslike' love-letters, only to be informed in her cool, controlled voice that one never knew into whose hands correspondence might fall, and then one would regret any indiscretion. There had never, so far as he could remember, been any indiscretion in any one of Ellen's letters, scarcely anything more incriminating than 'love, Ellen', neatly inscribed at the end.

This letter, apparently, was no different from any of the others. It began conventionally enough with a plain 'Dear Craig' and continued to say that she had thought she had, perhaps, been a little too precipitate in her arrangements for the future. She did not say so in actual fact, but Craig, reading between the lines, could see for himself she was presenting him, if he wished to accept it, with all the invitation possible without the actual words, with the opportunity for a reconciliation between them.

He folded the letter neatly and replaced it in the envelope. He was thoughtful, as he wondered what could have gone wrong with her plans where David Dearby and the combination practice were concerned. Something, he knew, must have upset Ellen deeply for her to write in this manner, for although she had not openly written a reconciliation would be acceptable, he knew her sufficiently well to realise the implication was there should he desire to take advantage of it.

The astonishing fact was that he had no desire to either see her or hear from her ever again. Even if, as he believed, Nona had found someone else and there was no hope for him there, he no longer wanted to take refuge in any engagement with someone else, not even with Ellen, to whom he had been engaged for such a long time. Knowing Nona had, he decided with a wry smile, told him what he had missed in his engagement to Ellen. He was in no hurry to put himself back into that position ever again! Unless, of course, the impossible happened and Nona tired of the young man he had seen her with that night . . . but they had seemed so happy, so very sure of themselves! It couldn't have been a *new* friendship! Nona, he was certain, wouldn't have quickly got on such friendly terms with just anyone, not after the shock her heart had received when her first love had jilted her.

"It must be someone she's known a long time," he told himself for at least the tenth time. "Someone she's turned to, perhaps after he's asked her out several times and she's at last gone with him . . . and was enjoying herself, as she's every right to do! How did *she* know what I think of her . . . she'd never have guessed I love her! I didn't know it myself until I found out she was with someone else and that I didn't mind about Ellen after all! I ought to have known," he blamed himself bitterly. "I ought to have realised how dependent I'd grown on her companionship, her friendliness. . . . Why didn't I know? Why didn't I realise what was missing whenever she wasn't there? I must have been too full of my own importance to even realise what she meant to me!"

He took out the letter, smoothed it and read it through again, noting facts which had escaped him previously. The marriage with David, he read, was postponed indefinitely, but there was no explanation as to the reason. Whatever it was, he told himself firmly, it had nothing whatsoever to do with him! He walked to the phone, intending to ring Nona and talk the matter over with her, but as his hand went out to the instrument he remembered how hurt she had looked in the theatre that afternoon when he had, merely to make certain no one had cause to say she was being singled out for special attention, reprimanded her on a very minor point, in front of the entire theatre staff.

His hand went to his side. Perhaps he was overdoing things a little, yet he knew he could no longer remain on the same friendly terms with her as previously. If he attempted *that*, he would find himself telling her what had happened between himself and Ellen, and why he was no longer regretful.

"I'll have to get her out of my system somehow!" he told himself, going back into the kitchen and making a determined attack on the cooking of his meal. "If I don't, or she doesn't marry and leave St. Jude's before long, I shall *have* to tell her, and knowing Nona, that'll make her unhappy when she realises she must choose between the bloke I saw with her and me!"

Over his meal he decided that perhaps she too was undecided as yet. She had seemed happy with the other man, certainly, and Nona wasn't the type to pretend. But so far there had been no talk of an engagement, no whisper along the grapevine as to Staff Hoyle's boyfriend or fiancée. Perhaps he was being a little too hasty in jumping to conclusions! He would wait until the next day, be more pleasant to her in the theatre . . . even though that would give rise, inevitably, to more and very real gossip! In fact, he resolved as he turned on the radio for the late-night news, he would be more pleasant to everyone tomorrow. Now he'd somewhat recovered from the shock of seeing Nona with another man he knew what he would do. He would . . . what was the old-fashioned word he wanted? He would . . . woo her, that was it. He would fuss over her, send her the flowers she loved so much she denied herself all sorts of small luxuries to provide herself with a costly bunch each week.

He'd buy her plants in pots, trinkets for the flat . . . he knew instinctively that, at least in the beginning, she wouldn't accept any gift for herself.

"I'll *court* her, as Mum's Sarah used to say," he grinned to himself as he switched off the light. "All's fair in love and war, they say, so I'll do my best."

Yet in the morning when he arrived at the theatre Nona wasn't there first as she usually was. Instead he was met with an annoyed Theatre Sister who informed him curtly, "My staff nurse has gone to see Matron, Mr. Roper. She has gone to ask if she may be transferred from theatre work for a time," and her attitude suggested most strongly that he was the person she blamed for this state of affairs!

CHAPTER 11

TO say that he was shocked by Nona's decision to leave theatre work if that were possible was to put the effect on Craig at its most minor point. At the time, and with a full list ahead of him, he could do no more than give Sister a curt nod as though he was aware of the state of things and was in full agreement. After that, as soon as Nona and the anaesthetist had settled themselves, he plunged into work like a man possessed.

Nona stole a covert glance at him from time to time. She had fully anticipated some form of rebuke because she had arranged to leave her position as Staff Theatre, but, so angry inside that he could not trust himself to speak, Craig merely nodded, giving her terse directions when he wanted to make known his requirements.

The list seemed endless. One perforated stomach resulting from a peptic ulcer; one partially strangulated hernia; one vagotomy, the first Nona had seen performed. There were several more minor operations, and all the time Craig worked as though he were completely automated. Nona seldom spoke in the theatre, only when absolutely necessary. That morning she did not speak at all, since to have said anything, she felt, would have been to invite Craig's displeasure, and after the rebuke of the previous day she felt she might very easily burst into tears if the same thing occurred a second time.

As soon as the last patient was wheeled carefully from the theatre, shrouded in his red blanket, Craig made all haste to scrub, change and depart. Normally he made a point of speaking to everyone concerned with the work of the morning, exchanging a pleasant word with each person, adding a hint of praise here, a word of appreciation there. This was one of the habits which everyone in St. Jude's in any way connected with the surgical side of the hospital felt endeared their new S.S.O. to them all. It had been such a pleasant change when Mr. Rawlingson had left, to work with someone who obviously did appreciate it took more than the S.S.O. to make a successful surgical team!

Nona watched him go and felt an ache in her heart almost as great as the relief which had swamped her being when they had reached the end of the list without his once saying anything to her which . . . *hurt*! Thank goodness, she thought as she looked round the theatre, mechanically made her checks and prepared to leave herself, Matron had not made any objections to her application for a transfer. She had looked up from the notes on her desk, he grey eyes serene and calm, and heard Nona out to the end.

"You feel you cannot do any more theatre work for the moment, Staff?" she repeated some of Nona's words out loud, nodding her head as though she quite understood. "I see. You've had a long spell there, I know, but I had thought things were . . . much less of a strain these days?" she concluded on a note of enquiry.

Nona nodded too, swallowing hard. That had been perfectly true, she felt, right up to yesterday!

"That is so, Matron," she heard herself giving the answer mechanically, "but I really *would* like a change, as soon as possible, please."

"I see," Matron said again, looking shrewdly into Nona's face. "Well, perhaps . . . Staff Casualty for a time? Nurse Benson is due for some leave, and perhaps that will be long enough for you to feel you can return to Theatre once she's back?"

"Thank you, Matron," Nona said, wanting to add that she didn't want to go back to Theatre until Craig was as he used to be, not if it meant going back on the wards, taking the Outpatients', *anything* but working where such close team co-operation was an absolute necessity!

"Nurse Lomax will relieve you, then," Matron ended the discussion, removing her notes and scribbling something on the side of her list. "From tomorrow morning you will be Staff Casualty, Nurse. That will be all."

That had been the end of the interview, but not, she thought now as she closed the main doors of the theatre, the end of the awful feeling for which there was no logical explanation, which seemed to grip her by the throat every time she thought of Craig Roper.

"Well," she told herself firmly as she walked briskly away from the theatre and then, seeing his broad-shouldered form at the other end of the corridor, turned and went the long way round by the longer external corridor, "I haven't done or said anything to upset him . . . not so far as I know! I wonder if Ellen has . . . ? But," she reminded herself bleakly, "he *did* say every thing had worked out quite satisfactorily, so *she* can't be responsible for this change that's come over him!"

Without turning round she could sense he had turned and was following, and she quickened her pace to the usual nurse's half run, half trot which enabled them to get from one part of the hospital to the other without running. Out of nowhere she remembered her first lesson in the correct demeanour of a nurse in hospital.

"No nurse," Sister Booth had intoned firmly, "runs unless in the event of fire or haemorrhage!"

Certainly the fact that the S.S.O. was obviously wanting to speak to the girl who, until this morning, had been his theatre staff nurse would not be looked upon by authority as anything in the least way resembling a crisis! She knew she was cheating slightly, but somehow she could not help herself. She simply didn't want to meet him just then, not without the mystery of his changed behaviour being first cleared up! As she neared the small door which led directly on to the covered way to the Nurses' Home she opened it and went through. He could not follow here, and she could always tell Home Sister she wanted to see Mavis Brommige, even though that meant the awful chore of thinking up, on the spur of the moment, something which would sound plausible enough to be poured into Mavis's eager ears.

She thought quickly. The nurses' carol service! That would be a wonderful excuse for a chat! Until she and Avice had taken the flat together Nona's clear soprano had been one of the mainstays of the St. Jude's nurses' choir. These past two years she had opted out, but all at once she wanted to be involved, to be part of any and everything that would be taking place at St. Jude's during the festive season. Yes, she congratulated herself, but there was no thrill in the congratulations, this would make the perfect excuse for seeking Mavis Brommige out for a chat!

Craig saw her disappear through the door and swore silently. It was more than obvious the move had been made to avoid a meeting with himself, but why?

"Maybe she thinks I was mad about her not being at the flat the other night," he reflected gloomily. "I can't tell her I'm not mad ... I wasn't *mad*, just plain more than disappointed. I can't tell her what did happen. Not now! I have some pride! She'll think I'm always running to her to patch up my love-life! And if she did but know it there's only one way in which she could do *that*, either now or in the future! I've been an idiot not to have known it before, and now it's too late! But not to have her in theatre, not working with her. . . ." He too turned on his heel and strode back the way he had just come, determined to return to the flat and try to reach her by telephone, once he had allowed her sufficient time to get home.

Nona did not hurry. Avice was on the last day of her split shift and wouldn't be in for some time. Normally Nona liked to have the flat to herself some of the time.

Avice was a good friend and a happy companion, but Nona liked reading, experimenting with her cookery and her flower arrangements and all the little domestic details which Avice found so boring or annoying. To-night, however, she felt she could not sit alone and wait until her friend came home.

She stayed as long as possible, spinning out the conversation and hoping Mavis hadn't guessed what she had come to say could just as well have been mentioned during a chance meeting in the staff canteen or anywhere else in the hospital they were likely to meet. Mavis, a gregarious creature, apparently looked upon Nona's visit as just a social call, and, when her visitor rose to go, chattered happily on: "It would be lovely to have you back in the choir again, Nona. Don't you feel it's a long trek back, though, after a day in the theatre? There never seems to be a slack period there!"

"I'm not in Theatre after today," Nona managed, though it felt strangely disloyal to have to say the words. "I'm Staff Cas from tomorrow morning! I asked for a change."

"You must be sickening for something, then!" Mavis laughed aloud. "I've only had small dealings with our new heart-throb, but I do know you've been the envy of all the nursing staff ever since he came! What happened? He hasn't done a Rawlingson on you, has he, and thrown something solid as well as a temperament?"

"Nothing like that." Nona hoped her smile did not look as sickly as it felt. "It's just . . . well, everyone needs a change of occupation every now and again," she said, forcing her tone to a brisk-sounding casualness she wondered might well never deceive anybody! "I expect I shall be going back after a spell away from Theatre."

"When's his supposed bride-to-be arriving?" Mavis pressed as Nona made a move towards the door. "I think she must be more than pretty sure of him to leave him at large like this, especially in a place like Whemlybridge!

I mean, it isn't just the hospital, is it? There are some pretty smart-looking girls in that new Governmental block of offices they've just opened on Morley Street! There are loads more, in and about the town, too. I saw a girl in Bab's Boutique the other day. She looked as though she'd stepped straight out of one of those glossy magazines, and she'd a car by the kerb, to match."

"Nice to be some people!" Nona said lightly, anxious to be on her way before the conversation somehow took on a more intimate note as conversations with people in the Nurses' Home were apt to do after a while. "See you, then," she called, starting down the corridor. "Eight o'clock Monday for a run-through? That right?"

"That's right," Mavis confirmed. "Now you're back we'll be able to do all the old numbers we used to do when you took the descant most of the time!"

Nona went slowly back along the external corridor, pausing en route to go into the cloakroom, because she had suddenly remembered there was a perfect view of the staff car park from the cloakroom window. She need not have worried, she told herself, and wondered a little at the forlorn feeling which seemed to engulf her at the realisation. Craig's Rover wasn't there. He must have turned in the corridor, decided whatever he had wanted to say to her wasn't really important and gone home. Gone to make more preparations for the arrival of the girl who, to quote Mavis, was more than pretty sure of of him.

She changed into her outdoor things, walked at a more leisurely pace than usual to the bus stop and did not even feel annoyed as the bus she intended to take pulled away from the halt as she almost reached the platform. Normally she would have sprinted after it, but today she simply sat in the shelter to await the arrival of the next one for her route. It was cold and there was a flurry of snow in the air. A woman entered the shelter, carrying a small girl, a boy a year or so older hanging on to her skirt.

"Soon be Christmas!" the woman remarked conversationally to Nona. "I always think it's the happiest time of the year, don't you?"

Nona nodded, but somehow she couldn't say the words. Until now, she thought, she too had believed the Christmas festival to be the "happiest time of the year," but not any longer!

"There's something . . . sort of magical about it, if you know what I mean!" the woman persisted. "Even the grumpiest of people seem to—well, mellow at Christmas-time!"

The grumpiest of people! The words repeated themselves in Nona's mind, even as she automatically answered her new companion. But Craig had been the least grumpy person she had ever known, until his visit to Emley and to Ellen!

"I think," she managed to get in a few words as the next bus stopped for them and the cheery conductress stepped down to help the woman and her children, "it's because it's really a children's time . . . and I don't just mean those who are children in years!"

For a second she thought the woman would think her completely mad, but her newly made friend smiled understandingly.

"For everyone who's a child at heart, you mean, don't you?" she said, opening her purse for her fare. "I do know what you mean. It's a long time ago, but when I was at school we were given a poem to learn and I've never forgotten it. It started with the words 'Know you what it is to be a child?' and went on to paint pictures of all sorts of delights we forget as we grow older. 'The world in a grain of sand,' as one line runs, and 'eternity in an hour.' Somehow, when I know they," she gave a significant smile at her two children, "are waiting to open their Christmas stockings, it must *seem* like eternity to them, waiting until we're ready to share the fun as we always do. That's the sort of thing I mean about Christmas. People *remember* what it was like to be a child, and that, I think, is what makes it so wonderful, so *magical*," she repeated the word as though she enjoyed saying it, "even though we all get older every year!"

"I think you may well be right!" Nona agreed as the bus halted at her stop. "It's been nice chatting to you. Happy Christmas, when it comes! 'Bye!"

The smile vanished from her lips as she went into Bannister's Ryde, but it was soon back in place when she reached her own floor and found two furniture men on the landing, a flustered Mr. Philip Horncastle attempting to direct operations and, at the same time, cope with the pretty young woman who was apparently his wife and who seemed to Nona's experienced eye to be on the verge of an outsize outburst of hysteria.

"Not there!" she was saying loudly as Nona stepped on to the landing. "It won't look right in that corner . . . it should. . . ."

"Doreen!" Phil ran a distracted hand through his hair. "Let them at least get the thing off the landing then people can come to and fro about their own business! We're causing enough trouble as it is. You mustn't have anyone telling the landlady we're a nuisance before we even *get* into the place!"

"Can I help, Mr. Horncastle?" Nona came forward quietly. "If your wife would care to come into our flat for a moment I'll pop the kettle on and soon have a nice hot cup of tea for you both . . . and," she smiled at the two moving men, "for these gentlemen as well."

"That's very kind of you, Nurse Hoyle," Phil Horncastle was beginning, but his wife caught Nona's name and interrupted quickly.

"*You* are Nurse Hoyle?" she began in a quick, nervous voice, introducing herself. "When Phil told me you had said you would vouch for us I just couldn't wait any longer. I telephoned the landlady from the kiosk on the corner where we used to live. She said if *you* vouched for us we were evidently all right, and told us we could move in right away, so here we are. If you'd be an angel and come and show me how this cooker thing works— it's so very different from the one in the old flat—I'll make the cup of tea here! It'll make me feel more at home quickly if I'm the one to be entertaining someone else!"

Why shouldn't she? Nona asked herself. There wasn't much point in sitting alone in *her* flat. Avice wouldn't be home for at least another hour and a half, and in her present state of mind that could well seem, to quote the woman from the bus, 'an eternity'.

"Time's really what's happening to you," she thought abruptly. "When you're happy, and everything's going right for you, time simply flies past. That's why I haven't noticed quite so much when we've been late finishing work in the theatre, not since Craig came! That's why the day he went to Emley seemed as though it would never end! And when it *did* end, I had to mess everything up like that!"

"Thank you," she smiled at Doreen. "If you're sure it won't be too much for you today! Entertaining someone, I mean, even to a cup of tea! Maybe there's something I can do to help, though. Let's have a look!"

She glanced out of the window, and away again. Foolish to expect to see Craig's car parked where he had parked it that night! Doreen, seeing her glance at the window, took it for granted that her new-found friend was looking for ways and means to help.

"The curtains are over here." She picked up a pile of gaily patterned material from a box standing in the corner. "I think they ought to fit, but I can't reach to hang them, and right now I somehow don't trust myself on the stool. I was waiting until Phil had finished helping the men get everything inside."

"We'll have them up in no time," Nona said cheerfully. "Look," she was standing by the stove, "you switch this thing here and that automatically lights the top. This," she touched another switch, "lights the oven, and here. . . ." She would, she thought with amusement, have been able to almost take a position as a gas-cooker demonstrator, except they probably had to take examinations in the making of various dishes which hadn't been on the cookery schedule when she had sat for her own G.C.E.

Doreen, happier now she had someone else in the flat with her, set to work with a will to make the promised cup of tea, talking all the time. She chattered with the aimless, rambling conversation of a person who has been lonely for some time and doesn't want to confess that as a truth. Nona could not help but feel that the move to this new home would be good for the girl in more ways than one. There weren't many days when both she and Avice were too busy or too dated not to have time to pop across the landing for a brief chat!

It would have been funny to think about dates in connection with herself, until a few short months ago, she realised. Now things were different, or *had* been different. She wasn't certain herself of how they were right at this moment. Craig, she felt, was tired of her company, perhaps embarrassed by the fact that she knew so much more than anyone else at Whemlybridge about his private life, and now regretted confiding in her at all.

That was why she had asked to be taken off theatre duty, although with her whole heart and mind she longed to be back there . . . but not unless there was a return to the easy companionship, the team spirit which had prevailed from the day of his arrival and lasted until he had returned to Emley for that brief visit. If her conjecture was the right one, she told herself as she listened with only half an ear to Doreen's chatter, leaving the theatre had been the only thing to be done. She could leave. Some other staff nurse would take her place, but not until the time for re-appointment, or only in the event of extremely unforeseen circumstances, would a new S.S.O. stand in Craig's place. And if I am right, her thoughts ran miserably, he won't really ever want to *see* me there again, much less have anything to do with me!

She couldn't have been more inaccurate in her thoughts, had she but known it. Craig had left St. Jude's, driven home and, not even bothering to eat or drink, gone at once to the phone to dial her flat number. He could hear the buzz, buzz, buzz of the number being rung out, but no one picked up the instrument.

"She can't have gone home," he thought gloomily, replacing his phone at last, "and her friend can't have got in yet either, or I'd leave a message!"

There didn't appear to be anything more he could do. He heated up his meal, ate in lonely silence until he could stand the quietude no longer and switched on the radio. Someone singing something about her love being blue made him switch stations rapidly, but here he fared no better, stumbling into a recital of Elizabethan love songs.

"They seem to have had a worse time of it than folks today," he reflected, switching the thing off altogether, but association of ideas made him remember how, in those times, so many people lost their heads—literally—because of a misplaced love affair, he decided that, after all, he was fortunate to be alive today!

"I'm not giving up without a fight!" he decided. "All right, so I was upset and ill-tempered yesterday and this morning. I think she should realise there's something wrong! I've never been like this in the theatre before . . . but I just couldn't think straight, seeing her out with that man! I mustn't be selfish. If she's found some-one else to take the place of Trevor or whatever his name was, then I must be as generously minded as she was. I must make friends with him. Get her to tell me about him as I told her about Ellen. One never knows, I may be able to help in some way," but his heart reminded him that in such an event he would be 'helping' her away from himself and the hoped-for opportunity of happiness together.

"If she'll stay in Theatre," he reasoned, "at least we ought to be able to remain friends! That's the main thing. If she goes off to some other part of the hospital more or less permanently, we shall never be the same again, and I don't think I can stand that! I'll go round to the flat and tell her," he decided. He'd tried to reach her in the hospital, and she'd fled. There had been no doubt about that! She'd seen him coming, and rushed into the Nurses' Home to avoid talking to him, and she herself had told him on more than one occasion she had been delighted to leave there and take up residence in her shared flat.

He made a final attempt to reach her by phone, but he didn't let the bell ring very long this time. There was no answer, and reluctantly he decided she either was out with the unknown man friend, or she was sitting reading, watching television or playing records and had decided not to answer the telephone in case it was himself!

He drove round to the flat, parking where he had parked on the previous occasion. There was no light in the girls' flat, but there was the bright one on the landing, shining through the slit window at the side, and another in the flat adjoining hers, the flat which had been empty. Perhaps, he thought happily, knowing how she loved to help everyone, she was assisting the new people, whoever they were, to move in. That was the sort of thing she would do, he told himself. That was why she hadn't heard the phone!

He crossed the road and entered the hallway, hurrying upstairs. The door of the flat adjoining Nona's was open, and it was obvious the young man staggering upstairs ahead of him under the weight of a large basket of crockery, was heading in that direction.

Craig halted in his hurry, pausing to watch the man round the curve in the stairway. There was something all too familiar about the set of the man's head, the shape of his shoulders, although the last time he had seen those shoulders, that head, the head had been thrown back against the wind and the shoulders had been clothed in an enveloping duffle coat or car coat!

It was the same man, he would have sworn to that on oath. As if to confirm his suspicions the man called: "This is the last load," and from somewhere in the flat Nona's voice called back: "Good. Tea's just poured."

He didn't wait to see her or to hear anything more. He rushed downstairs as though pursued by all the enemies he'd ever made or was likely to make for the rest of his life; across the road he ran, flinging himself behind the wheel just as Nona, showing how well she had managed to adjust the curtains in the flat, stepped across to draw them and to show Philip how well they hung.

CHAPTER 12

NONA stood with her hand on the curtain she was drawing across the window. There couldn't be a mistake! When she had looked previously there hadn't been a sign of any large car there, just a mini-something-or-other and the Fiat belonging to the man with the small grocer's shop on the corner. She stared as though mesmerised as the elegant Rover, with Craig at the wheel, began to edge its way out of the parking space. The light from the street lamp shone on him, and she had time only to see how strained and white-faced he seemed.

She was out of the flat and running downstairs as fast as her legs would carry her, almost upsetting the newly laid tea-tray which was precariously balanced on two packing cases until Doreen finally made up her mind which way round she wanted the small bookcase fitment.

It was too late. She saw the twin red rear lights disappearing towards the curve of the road. The left blinker blinked, and before she could possibly have even said his name, the car had disappeared from view and she was left disconsolately shivering in the cold night air.

She made her way slowly back up to the flat the Horncastles had taken. Phil, looking worried, met her at the door.

"Something wrong, Nurse Hoyle?" he queried. "You shot off before I had opportunity to ask if there was anything I might do to help."

"I . . . I thought I saw a friend of mine over the road, that was all," she said. Even her voice, she thought, sounded tired and dispirited now. "He'd gone before I got to the door. It doesn't matter. I wasn't expecting to see him, anyway, but when he was there. . . ."

The Horncastles looked at one another in bewilderment. Philip had never seen Nurse Hoyle with any man, and he had known her quite some time. He frowned warningly at his wife, knowing Doreen wouldn't think it in the least nosey or rude to ask questions. She would think only that it was merely kind to show an interest when she'd been so good to them, but somehow he didn't think quiet, self-contained Nurse Hoyle might look at things in the same light. To cover the momentary confusion he began to pour the tea, knowing perfectly well that the moment he did so Doreen would get up and take the tea-pot from him. She worried about her china, her small dishes, and was in constant dread that when the baby was born she would return from hospital to find the cupboard crammed full of the broken remains of the tea-set she had been given from the staff when she married, the odd remaining bits of the dinner-service the bank staff had contributed on their wedding day. She said now, taking the tea-pot from him: "I'll do this, love. You sit down. If Nurse had spoken instead of rushing off like that you could have gone down and *she* could have knocked on the window to attract her friend's attention. . . ."

"It really doesn't matter," Nona said quietly. "And he was in a car, anyway. He wouldn't have heard my knocking on the window, and I don't think he'll know your husband. It was . . . only someone from the hospital," she hated herself for that 'only,' but it was one way in which she hoped she could prevent Doreen making up romantic stories in her mind about what was, after all, an ordinary incident! "I shall see him in the morning, anyway."

"That's all right, then," Doreen observed comfortably. "Will you try one of these savoury scones? I got them at Blanchard's in the market."

Accepting, because it was easier than saying "No,

thank you" and then having to listen to Doreen's persuasions, Nona thought about the morning. She *might* see him, but again, it was highly probable she would not! Staff Casualty wouldn't have much to do with the S.S.O. unless something drastic had happened to a patient brought in by ambulance, and she hated that sort of thing to happen to anyone, even if it brought Craig into her orbit again, if only in his official capacity.

"I've *got* to see him now," she told herself. "I have to know what he was doing parked across there! He normally doesn't park anywhere near here if he's just going into Whemlybridge. He wouldn't come here unless there was something he particularly wanted to tell me, discuss with me. Perhaps about bringing Ellen to Whemlybridge! Maybe that's why he called at the flat so late the night he'd been to see her . . . I'll *have* to see him. I *have* to explain I wouldn't have asked to leave Theatre if he'd continued to be the same sort of person he's been since he first came here! It was only because he was so . . . angry, so sharply spoken with everyone —including me—that I knew I couldn't stand it any longer. I wish I hadn't asked to be moved now!" her thoughts ran on. "I ought to have remained the same, as I said I would. I didn't though! As soon as it seemed there was something else wrong I left him, almost ran out on him! It'll take some doing to swallow my pride enough to go to him and ask him."

She wasn't in the least sure *what* she could ask him as yet. It was one thing to make up her mind there must be a genuine reason for his coming to the flat and quite another to let him know that had been her presumption! What if he'd only been to the supermarket? She knew he shopped there sometimes, because she had told him of several of their special offers for late-night shoppers, and they had joked about it, comparing shopping lists.

She was never certain how she concluded the conversation with Doreen and Philip. She remembered saying to Doreen that if ever she needed her, or, in particular when the baby was due to arrive if she needed or wanted someone until the nurse, doctor or ambulance or taxi to take her to the maternity hospital arrived, she would come most willingly, if only she were not on duty.

She left with their grateful thanks still ringing in her ears and was just fitting the key into her own lock when she heard Avice run lightly upstairs.

"Not in yet, love?" Avice asked the obvious question. "Just as well," she continued cheerfully. "I took a chance you'd waited for me and, because it's my week for shopping and I'd just realised I'd nothing in the place except what took hours of cooking and fiddling about to do, I popped into Ramsdens and bought two hot pies, some chips and some hot peas!"

Nona shuddered, but laughed. There was always something surprising about Avice's culinary efforts.

"I thought you'd gone back on your diet?" she said, laughing. "That's the sort of thing to put weight on a skeleton!"

"It's only this once," Avice made her continued excuse. "I promise tomorrow I'll do something with that load of eggs I've asked them to deliver from the new dairy in Mythem Avenue. I'd had the man's wife in for a time, you know. Removal of a non-malignant tumour," she chattered on. "Anyone would think I'm the one to congratulate that the thing wasn't, as she thought it might have been, something really serious. She's so relieved she'd *give* me eggs and milk for months, if I could allow it. The only thing to do was to accept her offer of some at cost as she put it, so there'll be a crate or something arriving in the morning, and we'll be eating eggs and egg dishes until we both are ready to crow with delight."

"They're very good for us," Nona said almost mechanically. "Full of protein, vitamins, and non-fattening."

Her tone was so flat and she had not risen to the small

joke at all, as she usually did. Avice turned from the oven where she was deftly re-heating the pies, and stared at her friend.

"Something's wrong," she said firmly. "Come on, out with it! What's happened?"

"Nothing." Nona made an effort and tried to appear as though there was nothing at all wrong anywhere. She'd done this before, but strangely the memory was now a vague one instead of the painful reminder it once had been. That had been in the days following Trevor's letter, and it was then she had schooled herself into locking her grief, her hurt into her heart and presenting a quiet, calm face to the world in general.

"We can make omelettes," she said now, and saw Avice's blank stare. This time her laughter was genuine enough. "Haven't you heard the old saying?" she queried. " 'You can't make an omelette without breaking eggs.' If we're going to have plenty of eggs, then we'll have lots of omelettes. Savoury ones and sweet ones, filled and plain! An omelette's a versatile affair, and very good for you."

"A lot of things are very good for us," Avice was watching her closely, "but not all of them are pleasant!"

"You know I've asked to be released from theatre duty?" It was a statement rather than a question, and Avice nodded, listening.

"I'd . . . heard," she said slowly. "Why?"

"I thought I needed a change," Nona told her. "We . . . people get on one another's nerves working so closely *all* the time. . . ."

"And who's got on whose nerves?" Avice persisted, with a brutal frankness Nona herself could never have used.

"I don't quite know," she said thoughtfully. "All I know is that Mr. Roper's changed. Ever since he went to visit his fiancée he's not been the same person. What

154

was he like the night he called here, Avice? He'd just come back from seeing her then."

"Just the same as always," Avice chuckled. "I thought it might do him good to find out all the staff weren't as sold on the story of his devotion to this wonderful Ellen as you are! I tried to make him feel at home, fussed him a little, but he wasn't having any. As soon as he knew you were out he hopped it. Wouldn't even stay for a coffee or anything."

"You must have told him I wouldn't be long?" Nona asked, then, to Avice's relief, answered her own question disconsolately. "But I *was* a long time, wasn't I?" she remembered. "That was the night I met Philip Horn-castle and promised to try and help him. Then Peggy was going to phone her doctor. . . ."

"So you did your Florence Nightingale act all over again," Avice put in, "and what good did it do you? All that happened was by the time you phoned him he must have been in bed and just dropped off into a sound sleep! I don't wonder he was grumpy! All that driving in one day, no girl-friend coming back with him and his pal out when he called! Poor chap must have felt brushed off everywhere."

That must have been it. Nono told herself. Why didn't she think of all these things first, instead of jumping to conclusions and, because he had changed his normal charming manner for one of grim politeness, she hadn't swallowed it and waited for things to return to normal. No, she'd rushed off and asked Matron to relieve her of theatre duty, without so much as giving him the benefit of the doubt!

That settled it. She must see him now! She'd go an hour earlier in the morning and wait for his arrival. Her duty of Casualty didn't start until much later than she had been wont to begin work in Theatre. Night Casualty didn't go off until late because St. Jude's was one of the few hospitals trying out the new idea of dividing the night shift into two halves and the second person on didn't go off until ten o'clock, not having gone on until two in the morning.

Avice served the meal and, sensing Nona's reluctance to discuss either Craig or his affairs further, she broke into a new story about Sister Jarvis who, so the grapevine had it, was being seen about the town with Mr. Rempton, one of the directors at the new plastics firm which had just opened a second factory on the outskirts of Whemlybridge.

"Rutherford saw them at the Grand," Avice informed a disinterested Nona. "Not that Rutherford or her Harry can afford the Grand on their nights out, but they were passing, and they stopped to watch the neon Christmas sign they've just put up there. There's to be a Grand Ball," she quoted with emphasis, "on Christmas Eve, and another one, if you please, to 'See the New Year in at the Grand.' The tickets are thirty bob each for that one. I know, because Rutherford's pestering to go and she says Harry can't afford it. I should think not, indeed, if he's really buying her that special watch she said she was having as a Christmas present! She's the one who ought to have managed to get off with Mr. Rempton! After all, he was only in for observation. I wouldn't have thought gratitude to Sister went as far as that!"

"And you with a crate of eggs as a result of someone's sheer relief!" Nona laughed. "I like people to be thoughtful, though," she continued reflectively. "They must realise, many of them, what we all do for them while they're in hospital is much more than just a duty! I think that's true of all the staff at Jude's."

"I think it's true of most of the professions," Avice, for once, was completely serious. "Medical staff as well as nursing staff, I mean. None of us would do it, otherwise."

"That's true." Nona agreed, but once again her tone was almost mechanical. Mentally she was rehearsing what she could say to Craig Roper the following morning to break down this barrier which had arisen between them. Nothing she thought of seemed to be any use. She tried a variety of approaches, mentally.

"I thought you might be upset because I wasn't at the flat when you came back from Emley. . . ."

That sounded as though she felt he had prior claim on her off-duty time and a *right* to her attention whenever he demanded it. She knew he didn't think of her along those lines, if indeed, she thought wryly, he thought of her at all!

"You seemed so . . . different, to all of us, after you came back from Emley. You were short and sharp with everyone. . . ."

That was impossible, too. He was under no obligation to be polite and friendly to anyone at St. Jude's. It was simply that they were all so accustomed to Mr. Rawlingson's autocratic and antagonistic manner it was just as great a shock to find Craig rivalling him as it had been to find him so amiable!

"I thought a change from theatre work would be good for me. . . ."

He would know, immediately, that was untrue. More than once he had remarked on her excellence as a theatre staff nurse, and she had always responded by saying, truthfully, that she loved her work. It wasn't reasonable to suppose she would change just like that, almost overnight, as it were.

Avice, after several fruitless attempts to engage her in any sort of a conversation, whether gossipy or otherwise, had given up talking and turned on the television, watching as she sped in and out with dishes.

"I'm going to the Swinging Lantern," she confided, naming the new discothèque which had opened a week previously. "Want to come along? The change will do you good. Joan's getting ready to go off to her aunt's tomorrow, so she won't be coming. It's her vac, anyway.

She can't go home because her two young sisters have measles. I don't want to go with Ron and Peter on my own, so I said I'd find someone else to accompany Pete. I've half asked Sandra Lewis, but she won't mind if I phone the Home and. . . ."

"Don't do that, please!" Nona said quickly, too quickly, she decided seeing Avice's suspicious glance. "I've a headache." She fell back on the age-old female excuse, but this time it was true. Her head *did* ache, abominably, but normally she'd have swallowed a couple of aspirins and tried to forget it, as Avice well knew. "I think I'll make a cup of tea and go to bed early. Perhaps it's the thoughts of the change I'm making. Cas. is somewhat different from the theatre, you know."

"Can't see why you wanted to make the change myself," Avice said. "You've always been as devoted as any surgeon to that theatre, said it was your hospital life and all that rot! I always felt you got too involved in what went on there, even when we'd Rawlingson to contend with. Now, when there's somebody there you like and get along with, you're not satisfied! You ask to be relieved . . ."

"Oh, leave it alone for a minute, can't you?" Nona was exasperated more than she would have believed it possible to be by such a trivial thing. Avice stared in astonishment for a full minute, then she smiled, an understanding smile which said more plainly than words could have done that all was forgiven.

"You really have a bad head, haven't you, love?" she said with deep sympathy. "I'll make your tea. You go and lie down for a while and I'll pop in with it before I leave. Poor old you!" she gave her usual merry grin. "And there I was thinking you were doing your old act of leaving everything and everybody because something had gone wrong with your own private little world! I couldn't have been more wrong, could I? Sorry! You pop into bed and I'll bring a couple of aspirins too! You ought to try and get some sleep. You'll probably feel a great deal better by morning!"

Nona knew there was little point in arguing. She went into her bedroom and undressed, climbing into bed and feeling a dreadful fraud. Yet somehow there was comfort in the warmth of the bottle Avice brought moments later, in the shaded light, the silence of the flat as Avice, with a final "Cheerio, see you soon. Hope you'll feel better," banged her way out to her evening of pleasure.

Nona pulled the bed-covers about her shoulders and settled down to try and sleep, but first, she resolved, she must decide what she intended to say to Craig in the morning. She tried. She tried very hard, over and over again, but it was all no use. Whatever she thought she would be able to say seemed totally inadequate, simply, she felt instinctively, because none of it was the truth. The truth was plain and simple. She felt that *he* felt she had failed him, and that he resented that failure. Yet she couldn't be sure, wouldn't ever know unless he too broke down his guard and told her what it was he had called to discuss with her the night he returned from Emley!

She tossed and turned despite her headache, but sleep would not come, and she was dozing off into an uneasy slumber when Avice returned, cheerful as always, and immediately contrite because she thought she had wakened Nona. At least, Nona reflected, she was able to say with truth, her headache had eased considerably and she felt very much better. Avice made a light supper and insisted on carrying a tray in to her friend, chatting all the time about her evening. By the time she had eaten her supper and listened to her friend Nona was indeed feeling sleepy, and to her relief, shortly after Avice went to her own room, she felt her eyelids close and she drifted into a sound and relaxed slumber.

Next morning she was awake early. She made the breakfast and ate her own before calling Avice, about two seconds before her alarm clock sounded its warning.

"You needn't have bothered, love," Avice protested, "not that it isn't lovely to have breakfast in bed occasionally, but you weren't well last night. What's wrong this morning? Haven't you slept well after all?"

"Like a top, thanks," Nona smiled. "I'm going early." She did not want to spend a long time in involved explanations. "I've things to see to before I start my day."

"Choir and all that, I suppose," Avice murmured, settling down again for a further five minutes. "Set the clock again, will you, pet? You've saved me a mad rush. I'm going to sneak that extra five minutes in bed by way of a change. See you tonight!"

The bus was crowded and, it not being her usual time for leaving, she found she had to stand most of the way because the vehicle had already almost filled before it reached her stop. Changed and walking down the corridor which led to the theatre, she felt a moment of panic. What if the others were there already? They should be, but she was counting on Craig's customary practice of parking his car, on busy mornings, on the small park just beyond the theatre and used generally only in emergencies or when the theatre staff were rushed. Careful enquiries had elicited the fact that there was an even longer list than usual, so it was more than likely he would come in this way and she would be able to see him before he reached the doors to the main theatre.

She was in luck. She heard him slam the door of his car and seconds later she heard his unmistakable step along the corridor. It took a great deal of effort for her to move out from the alcove which she had chosen as a refuge. For some reason her mouth was dry and she felt that, unless she were very careful, her hands and her voice would shake and reveal the extent of her nervousness.

Craig halted at the sight of her standing there. Most of his mind wanted to tell him to move forward, to put his arms about her and to tell her he hoped she'd changed her mind and was coming back to theatre work immediately. The remainder of his intelligence told him that would at once put them back on the old footing, and that wasn't fair to Nona if she really was interested in the young man she'd been with that night, the young man who, it seemed, had now moved into the next-door flat!

"You're somewhat out of your orbit for these days, aren't you, Staff Hoyle?" he asked in a cold tone. "I didn't know they'd moved Casualty down here?"

"I'm not . . . I mean, they haven't. I mean . . . I wanted to see you," Nona said in a breathless little rush. "I thought I saw you in your car opposite Bannister's Ryde last night. I wanted to know if you'd been to our flat. Avice is on split shifts—or was—and wasn't home, and I'd just passed into next-door. . . ."

"I don't see any reason to suppose I had been to call on you, do you, Staff?" he enquired still coldly. "If you must know where I'd been I had been to the shops. I won't use that parking space again if it upsets you."

"It doesn't . . . I mean, you have a right to park where you like, or where you can," she said confusedly. "It isn't any of my business, I know. I just thought if you *had* called. . . ."

"I can think of no reason why I should have called on you, can you?" he flicked the onus back on to her quickly, and, blushing, she could not even think at all. All she was conscious of was the tone of his voice, a tone which seemed to say, as plainly as words could have done, that she would be the very last person in the world upon whom he would call now or ever again.

"I'm sorry," she said quietly, turning to go. "I apologise. It was simply that I thought. . . ."

"I know what you thought." Craig too was nearly at breaking point. "You've already told me."

Nona said nothing more. She turned and, ignoring the rules about nurses not running in the hospital, she ran as fast as she could until she reached Casualty block.

All day, as she worked, the words he had said and the tone in which he had uttered them returned to taunt and to haunt her, burning bitterly in her heart. She worked as she always worked, but her heart wasn't in what she was doing. All she wanted to do was to hide away, anywhere where no one knew her. When she had been jilted by Trevor she had been hurt, she remembered, but not like this. This was like dying a slow death, a death by torture, and there was no relief, none at all.

She'd go away, she told herself as the day wore on and Casualty Sister asked if she were ill. She'd hand in her notice, although how she would stay until she had worked the required length of weeks, she just didn't know.

She'd go off sick, but the R.M.O. would know there was nothing wrong with her. Nothing he could do anything about, that was. Who could do something about it, and what *was* wrong with her? She asked herself that question on and off throughout most of the day, and she was still trying to make up her mind exactly what it was as she went upstairs to the flat.

She prepared the meal, pottered about, and all the time she was picturing him sitting in the chair he always favoured when he had visited them. Her chair . . . Nona's chair, as the girls called it to themselves. She didn't even need to close her eyes to see him as he had sat there on the occasion of his first visit, worn and strained and . . . shocked.

Her face was white and there were dark circles beginning to show beneath her eyes by the time Avice came home, her cheery greeting stilled as she looked at her friend.

"Still got a headache, love?" she enquired anxiously. "Have one of these," she shook two pellets from a bottle in her handbag. "Your friend Craig left them here the last time he called. I've been meaning to see he had them back some time, but . . . here," her voice rose, "what's the matter?" for without any warning, at the mention of his name and of his last visit to the flat, the visit when she hadn't been there still the same as she had promised, and from which time everything in her world seemed to have gone wrong. Nona's head had gone down on her arms and she was crying as though her heart was broken.

Puzzled, Avice laid a friendly, comforting hand on her shoulder, wondering if she were sickening for the influenza which was sweeping the township. This, she felt, was something more than an influenza bug, distressing though that might be. She went down on her knees beside the other girl and pulled Nona's face to her own.

"Tell me," she urged gently. "Tell me what's wrong."

It was a relief to talk about it at last. Without even considering her words Nona's story spilled out into Avice's willing ears.

"I thought I loved Trevor Brady," she sobbed quietly. "I didn't. I know now I was just in love with love, and that's an altogether different thing! I'd give *anything* to help Craig with whatever bothered him that night, and something must have done, because he's not been the same to anyone since! That was why I asked to leave theatre work. I couldn't stand it when he began behaving like Mr. Rawlingson! I'd go back if he wanted me, of course. But he doesn't. He doesn't want to have anything more to do with me at all! And I don't know why!"

She broke into sobs again and Avice hushed her, gently, soothingly as one would attempt to soothe a child, and gradually the sobs grew quieter and Nona began to relax.

Not so Avice. Now, she felt, *she* knew what was wrong, but she did not dare to put her feelings into words. If she were wrong she wouldn't improve matters, only make them worse! If she had not told Craig Roper Nona had gone out with someone else he might have waited for her, might never have snapped at her when, eventually, she had telephoned him!

"He'll think she was out with someone else all that time," Avice realised. "And now it's too late . . . if I went to him and told him the truth I doubt if he'd believe me! He's proud and she's proud. Where do we go from here?"

CHAPTER 13

ELLEN stood by the window of the waiting room in the large airy surgery belonging to the combined practice where David Dearby was the most junior partner. With all her heart she prayed that no one, least of all David himself, would ever realise the shock which had gone through her when he had confessed his desire to emigrate.

"I shall earn twice the money, Ellen," he said, *insisted*, almost in despair in the face of her continued opposition. "It isn't as though either of us is too old to fall in with the ways, manners and customs of a new country. It's people like ourselves they *want* to take up positions with them. There's a crying need for our sort of people over there!"

"There's what you call 'a crying need' for doctors and nurses here as well!" she had returned, but her pride would not allow her to voice her innermost thoughts. What, she wondered, would she have to face in a strange hospital in a strange country? Nursing could well indeed be the same the world over, but the customs of the hospital, the ways of the staff—*everything* would be different, and she knew she was not sufficiently brave to accept that challenge.

"For chicken feed!" David had retorted immediately, and gone on to contrast the salaries of the two men who had left Emley General, one for Canada, the other for Australia, only two years previously with his own immediate remuneration and possible prospects. "In two years," he had concluded, "we could be living an entirely different life. We'd have new friends, new interests, more money to spend and more leisure in which to enjoy it. Right now I'm not worried that we have the most marvellous Health Service in the world! That's fine, but it's not enough for me. I want freedom to be myself, freedom to live a life where I have some extra time to spend with my family, and where I shall have money to enjoy all the things I've earned in this life. Think it over, Ellen, and I'm sure you'll agree with me."

He'd gone out then, on his morning round. He would be back at any minute, and within half an hour he'd be taking the morning clinic, ante-natals in the first hour, post-natals in the second.

"And afternoon surgery for those who can't get in the evening, after luncheon," her thoughts ran on. "Another runaround to those he hadn't managed to contact that morning or whose calls had come in after his morning list had been made out. Then evening surgery, and maybe some late calls to very sick people. That's the way it goes, even in a practice this size!"

She moved restlessly away from the window. What did she really want? It wasn't like Ellen to ask herself this question. Usually she knew what she wanted and strained every nerve to attain it! That, she reflected now, was the way in which she had got Craig Roper, only he, poor dedicated pet, hadn't seen it quite like that!

Her thoughts went back to the day she had first met him. Even at that first meeting she was certain here was a man who would go far in his profession. It hadn't been easy to get to know him. He lived for his work, and had little or no interest in her sex. The only way in which she could hope to attract his attention, she realised quickly, was by an equal devotion to her own work . . . and to him! It had begun more or less as a game, a game of which she seemed never to tire. She was always appearing where he was, or was likely to be. Always, of course, by accident. No one but Ellen knew how carefully most of those 'accidents' had been contrived!

She had been especially careful not to obtrude her own thoughts, her own ideas, but rather to fall in with his

166

own. Day by day he grew to trust her, to depend on her appearance at the staff canteen when he entered, on her being at the library when he went in search of a particular book on his own subject, at the special 'extra' voluntary lectures. She hadn't been in love with him, but she had been fond of him, proud of him, and proud of the fact that . . . one day she would stand beside him in the beautiful home he was, by this time, always planning. They would have the perfect family, the ideal family life. They would be accepted socially. People who now thought of her as simply 'Nurse' would refer to her as 'Mrs. Roper, the consultant's wife, you know.'

The dream had seemed perfect, but never seemed to come any nearer to becoming a reality. Then David had come to the hospital one day, accompanying a patient.

It would have been wrong to say she had fallen in love with him either. Craig had gone to Whemlybridge for his interview, and she was somewhat at a loose end. When David had invited her out that evening she had consented, a little amused that someone other than Craig should issue such an invitation. It wasn't until much later that she remembered every other male on the staff regarded her as Craig's property, and therefore not to be invited out solo.

David had more than invited her out. He had taken her to the small but exclusive Pagoda restaurant, the latest thing in Emley, and afterwards driven her home, gone in for coffee and stayed talking, talking for hours.

Craig never had time to talk, not these days. She and David, it seemed, had discussed everything, from the type of home they would want if and when they married—and discovered tastes very similar in consequence—to their ideal meal on a slender budget. Ellen hadn't even thought about which way her ideas were leading her until, some weeks after Craig had installed himself in the huge house he had apparently purchased, David, sharing a meal in her rooms, had astonished her by a sweeping proposal of marriage.

Thinking about it now she realised what had happened. With Craig there was always talk of 'when we've done this' or 'after we've achieved that.' David had no such idea. David's idea was to do the thing *now*, not to waste all their lives waiting for an opportunity which might never come.

She had thought the opportunity of a junior partnership in the practice would have contented him, and so it had done, until that letter had arrived from his friend in Canada. Perhaps it was fate, she reflected, perhaps it was simply blind chance, but when one of his patients, an elderly spinster in the town, revealed that she too had received a letter from the other doctor who had gone to Australia and who had travelled on the same boat as the spinster's brother, it had seemed the last straw.

David had been amazed at first, then envious, openly and frankly envious of the two men, qualified as he himself was qualified, and yet apparently leading such fulfilled and well-paid, interesting lives. It was then the battle had begun, she remembered.

She turned away from the window and the restless playing with the cord of the venetian blind which shrouded it, in summer, from the direct sunlight. Where David wanted to go, she reflected, the sun would be strong, and the colours of the furniture, the fabrics, geared to cope with its hotter rays.

That was partly why she was afraid. The English climate might, most of the time, be a target for jokes, an irritation with which one grew to live, but at least it was never so extreme—or rarely so—that its moods could distress, even kill.

"I'm a coward!" she thought soberly. "That's what's been the matter all the time! If I'd told Craig I really didn't mind being poor so long as he went ahead I'd do my best to prepare myself to keep pace with him mentally and all that, he *might* have taken a chance earlier. We might have married, had a home, no matter how small, and a family. I could have lived out—gone private nursing part-time or something like that, there's always scope! He could have lived in hospital as he's done right up to going to Whemlybridge, and we could have gone there *together*, as a complete family unit, but I was afraid he might refuse."

She hadn't been afraid to face the difficulties of being poor or living separate lives, she knew. She had been afraid to pit her will against his, because, she faced the thought honestly now, there hadn't been any real love between them.

"He wasn't even . . . upset when he came to see me last," she thought bitterly, remembering. "I can't understand it . . . except that providing anything didn't interfere with his precious career he never seemed to take very much notice! It must have been that! He can go on alone, independently. It ought not to be too difficult to convince him we could manage better together . . . now that I've had second thoughts."

Her reverie was interrupted by David's return. He looked tired, she thought abruptly. She could well understand his desire for a little greater reward for his endeavours!

"Cup of tea?" she asked automatically, switching on the kettle as he nodded. "There's just time before clinic starts."

"The first appointment's in five minutes," David glanced at his watch and took a mouthful of the hot, sweet, stimulating tea. "Just time to let me know what you're going to do. *I'm* posting this letter off as I finish. It asks 'married or single.' Which shall I fill in? It's up to you, remember. I've made up my mind. I'm going, anyway."

"Then there's no more to be said," Ellen said quietly. She was still as outwardly cool and composed as ever. It had taken her years to acquire that exterior poise, and now it was instinctive, never deserting her, not even in a moment such as this.

"Take the afternoon off—if anyone says anything tell 'em I've asked Nurse Taylor to step in, I said you weren't feeling too good—and think it over," David offered, watching her with a troubled gaze. He was a little in awe of this cool, pale, composed girl he believed he had swept off her feet. He'd been wrong, he admitted to himself now. Ellen's feet were planted firmly on the soil of 'what's best for Ellen,' and nothing, he knew now, would move them. "I'll post it by second post."

"I'd post it now, if I were you," she said, still quietly. "I *will* take the afternoon off, but you needn't have lied for me! I feel fine, in fact it's a long time since I felt so well and alive. I'm going to Whemlybridge. I can get a train at half-two and be in there by five."

"If you're thinking of contacting your ex-fiancée," she had not known David's voice could sound so brutal, so uncaring, but she had not realised the blow she had unwittingly dealt his own pride by her refusal to even consider accompanying him, "I wouldn't bother if I were you! He's found someone else. John Lewisham, you know, the E.N.T. man, was talking about it in the club the other night. Some Staff Nurse Hoyle or other. She's Staff Theatre there, and it seems she means much more to him than *that*! Apparently he's always round at her place. . . ."

Ellen stood still. She could not have moved had her life depended upon doing so. This was something she hadn't ever imagined to be even remotely possible. Craig and another woman . . . girl, if she were a staff nurse. Ellen could picture her, another tall, competent blonde with a complete devotion to the man and to his work. A 'yes, sir' woman! She knew the kind!

"I shall go, just the same," she said quietly. "Don't forget," she hoped she might be forgiven for the outright lie, "Craig has bought a house . . . we haven't managed to settle whose money is involved so far! That's reason enough for contacting him, I think."

"You saw him a few weeks ago," David countered suspiciously, but she wasn't to be drawn. She shrugged her shoulders indifferently as though the matter were no further concern of hers, and turned away.

"Everything's ready for Elsie," she said in a flat tone, and blessed the idea, whoever had thought of it, of a relief nurse always to hand.

She made an unhurried way home, bathed, changed and put on her clean dress and make-up with more than her customary care. She took a taxi to the station, an unheard-of luxury where Ellen was concerned, but she was determined to arrive on time and completely un-flustered. All the way along the journey she mentally reviewed how she might approach Craig in the most convincing manner. Her letter, and her cheeks burned at the memory of the words she had written, had brought no response whatsoever. At the time, whenever she had hurried to see what letters the postman had brought, she had decided he was much too busy in his new appointment to have found time—or energy—to write. David's words about a Staff Nurse Hoyle had made her think differently altogether. This was some-thing tangible, something she would have to fight if she were ever to regain the comfortable world of being the fiancée of Craig Roper, the up-and-coming consultant surgeon of the future!

By the time the train drew in at Whemlybridge station she had decided what she must do, and lost no time in putting her plan into action. David had said 'he's always round at her place,' therefore it was more than obvious that the girl did not live in the Nurses' Home!

She fumbled in her purse for the necessary coin, having first looked up the number in the directory. From the hospital switchboard she asked to be put through to the Home, and when the telephone was taken over by Home Sister she was ready.

"I am looking for a friend of mine," she began in her most friendly, modulated tones, "a Staff Nurse Hoyle. I'm told she is on the staff of St. Jude's, but I am only here for the day and unless I can get in touch with her immediately I shall have to leave without seeing her. I wonder if you could help me, please? May I leave a message. . . ?"

The reply was exactly what she had hoped it would be. She was told quietly and firmly that Staff Hoyle did not live at the Home, but had a flat she shared with another staff nurse at Two A Bannister's Ryde!

Ellen thanked Home Sister gravely and hung up. It would have been too daring—and no part of her plan—to find out whether or not the girl was still on duty.

She glanced at her watch. Theatre staff would be changing over any time now, and the emergency night staff taking over in case of unforeseen catastrophes of the night. She took another taxi and went out to Bannister's Ryde, surprised to find the flats in such a pleasant area. She paid off the man and walked across, up the stairs to the door of flat Two A. Although she hadn't decided what she meant to say to the girl she hadn't the faintest doubt but that the right words would come when she needed them, the words which would be most effective, help the girl to see that an engagement of such long standing as hers and Craig's had been wasn't to be dismissed lightly by one or the other of the parties having a spate of 'last-minute' nerves! That was what she was going to use, she told herself, pressing the bell firmly. No one could dispute her! They'd have to accept her word.

Avice had been enjoying her free day. To her astonishment, and, secretly, her delight, Ron was beginning to be really serious in his intentions. At first she couldn't believe her luck, then only two days ago he had fixed up to take her to meet his parents in the two free days she would get over the Christmas vacation! Fired by the scent of Nona's baking the previous evening, she had asked, humbly for her, for a simple recipe to try out on her free day and Nona, delighted, had left her an outline of a simple meal she was cooking for the two of them, and to which—daringly—she had added a small amount of her own ideas with regard to a sweet.

When the doorbell rang she gave one calculating glance at the clock, then—in case it might be Doreen and she would be away some time—took out her Saffron Delight and put it on to the wire tray to cool.

To Ellen, looking expectantly upwards, the sight of the mass of flaming red-gold hair, the slanting green-grey eyes with their long lashes, was so utterly unexpected that she was, for the moment, speechless. When she had recovered sufficiently from the shock she asked nervously:

"Staff Nurse Hoyle?" and wasn't sure whether to be relieved or worried by Avice's shaken head.

"Not back yet," she said crisply. "I'm her flat-mate, Nurse Foyly. Can I give her a message?"

"Will she . . . is she likely to be out long?" Ellen asked, not quite daring to ask whether or not Staff Hoyle might be out for a meal somewhere . . . with Mr. Roper.

"She'll be in by eight-thirty, I expect," Avice opined, adding, "but I don't know how long she'll be in for. Who shall I say called?"

"Sister Ellen Drayton, from Emley," Ellen said quickly, and knew the moment the words had left her lips she had made a grave mistake. She saw Avice's interest quicken, knew the girl knew all about her and the long—the too-long—engagement between herself and Craig.

"I see." No one could have drawled the words in a more insulting tone than the one Avice used at that moment. Outwardly she was calm, inside her brain was racing. It was plain to see why this woman had called!

She was going to try and trick Craig Roper into taking her back, back to an engagement Avice was by now certain he didn't want. She was as certain now that he loved Nona as she was in her knowledge of Nona's own confession that she loved him, and she, Avice, had been the means of separating those two who, she was now convinced, were made for each other.

She had been given an opportunity to repair the damage she had done the night he had returned from Emley, and she would take it with both hands, hoping and praying all would yet come right for her friend, and for the man to whom she had given her heart.

"I said I didn't know how long she would stay in," she murmured as though thinking back to arrangements previously made. "She and Mr. Roper may well go on to the house . . . it's a big one on Oakfield Avenue, you know. It's called Grey Walls. Once there I wouldn't know what time they'll be back, there's such a lot to be done, you know."

She hadn't *said* they were preparing to live in it, together. She hadn't *said* they would leave the hospital together. She had merely *implied* what she hoped Ellen would assume, and that was all. "Would you like to come in and wait?" she opened the door invitingly, "or to leave a message?"

"No. No, thank you." Ellen could sense the girl's antagonism from where she stood. If this was what she must expect from the friend of the girl who'd attracted Craig, then what she could expect from the girl herself *or* from Craig she couldn't imagine! "Don't tell them . . . anything," she said tonelessly. "Not even that I called. I'll . . . write when I get back. Good-night."

"Good-night," Avice called, and bit back 'and a merry Christmas.' She hadn't liked what she had seen of Ellen, the cold, proud beauty, the sense of believing herself to be a superior being which emanated from Ellen almost without her knowledge. Yet, quite unexpectedly, she felt sorry for her; then, being Avice, she shrugged her expressive shoulders, went inside and shut the door.

Ellen went slowly downstairs. She had failed. Whoever this unknown Staff Hoyle was it was plain that she and Craig must be almost on the point of marriage, even to the extent, she shuddered, of their choosing together the decorations and furnishings of the house she had never even troubled to come and see. At the time she had thought it would be like so many of the things she and Craig had planned, a dream to fulfil when he had the time. She had ignored his letters, phone calls, his impassioned pleas to come and see for herself, to have some share in the planning of the home they had hoped to inhabit together. Now he had found someone else to share it with him, and she was too late!

She could *see* it, though! Perhaps even catch a glimpse of Craig himself, and of the girl, if she went now and stayed in a taxi outside the house. It would be an expensive way in which to see the house which had been intended as her own home, but it was the only one. She couldn't afford a great deal on paying the taxi to wait outside until they arrived, but, she set her lips in the firm line her nurses knew so well, if that was the *only* way, then she must do just that!

She crossed to the taxi rank where she had left her cab which had brought her from St. Jude's. There was no difficulty in finding one to take her to Grey Walls, Oakfield Avenue.

"Mr. Roper's house, lady?" the driver asked. "Hop in. Don't think he'll be home yet by all accounts, busy up at Jude's they are just now, but we'll see. . . ."

Ellen set her teeth and listened as he talked on. Craig, it appeared, was popular in the town. He had operated on the driver's brother six weeks before. The wife of the driver had a sister—or some such tangled definition which escaped her at the moment—who'd been a patient of his.

175

"Like going to a friend for help, an' like a friend comin' round to see after you, if you get what I mean," the man chatted on. "Not a bit like it was when the other bloke was there, Rawlingson, his name was. . . . Nobody liked him."

Ellen let him talk on, saying a conventional 'oh,' or 'fancy that' at irregular intervals, and all the time she was watching, as well as she could in the darkness of the December evening, the type of area in which he had chosen this house . . . *their* home to be, now his and that of the unknown Staff Hoyle!

" 'Ere we are, miss." The cab drew up with a flourish outside the neat gates of a charming, well built house, attractively painted, as she could plainly see for herself by the light of the decorative mock gas-lamp (the old-fashioned kind which Craig loved) which stood, lit now by electricity, in the garden.

She got out of the cab and walked to the gate. Even under its powdering of snow the garden looked huge and attractive, tree-lined. There were attractive curtains at the windows of the house too, and she wondered vaguely if their colour and pattern had been Craig's choice or that of the unknown Nurse Hoyle.

She wouldn't, *couldn't* be caught snooping! She turned swiftly as there was the sound of a big car coming down the avenue. The cab stood at the gate, but she would be seen if she went across the road and hid under those shadows until they had gone indoors. They'd only see the driver and his empty cab and conclude that his fare was visiting the other, the brightly lit house a little further on. And if the driver thought her mad, well, that was his business! At the moment she didn't care what anyone thought of her. Her one idea was to see, with being seen, to know for herself what this other girl was like, the one who, in such a short time, had supplan her in Craig's affections.

She did not hear the warning shout of the driver. She

had been so certain this was *his* car, coming to halt by *his* gate that it had never occurred to her that it might well be the car of someone else going further down the avenue.

The driver of the oncoming car, seeing the standing cab and knowing Craig Roper not to be at home at this time on any night, had no idea of someone about to hurtle across the road from in front of the parked cab and directly in the path of his own wheels. The right-hand wing had struck her before he had really been aware she was there, and all Ellen was conscious of was that it wasn't Craig after all, but an unknown and very worried middle-aged man who helped the driver carry her into the cab, then darkness descended on her and she had no idea that, after all, she was being driven nearer and nearer to the two people she had striven so hard to see.

CHAPTER 14

ELLEN recovered consciousness as she was lifted from the ambulance. The hospital was strange, unfamiliar, but the entrance differed in scarcely any way from the entrance to Emley General, so that, for a brief bewildered moment, she felt herself at home. Her clouded mind fastened on two words, words which she was not yet certain hadn't indeed been spoken by herself.

"Staff Hoyle," she heard someone saying, over and over again, and then she *was* certain. That was her voice. It was herself, asking for the unknown nurse in whom Craig was interested.

Someone bent over her, spoke soothingly as she herself had so often spoken to patients brought into hospital as she herself had been brought in.

"Staff Hoyle will be along in a moment," a voice said. "She was just going off duty. Lie still, she'll be here in a moment."

Ellen obediently lay still. She was aware of movement all about her, of people coming and going, and a subdued sense of activity such as one often sensed in such places. She closed her eyes and, seconds later, was aware of someone standing close beside her, looking at her.

Ellen looked up. It was an effort, but she had to know. She almost laughed aloud as she saw Nona's serene young face looking into her own, almost but not quite. There was something so reassuring in the slim, cool hand, the firm yet delicate touch, the serene but strangely sympathetic eyes and in the quiet, calm young mouth which defied her laughter. Already she knew, without a word being spoken between them, what the quality was in Nona Hoyle which Craig evidently found so attractive.

"I hear you were asking for me," Nona said gently. "What can I do for you?"

Ellen lay in silence. This wasn't someone to fight. The other girl, the one who had been at the flat, she could have fought her and enjoyed the battle, but this girl . . . never.

"I'm . . . my name is Ellen Drayton," she said almost in a whisper. "From Emley."

Nona was absolutely astounded, but it would have comforted her to know that no one, least of all Ellen herself, could have guessed, so quietly and, apparently, so full of acceptance did she stand there.

"I see," she said, and smiled, the slow, warming smile which had first made Craig see her as someone different, the smile which turned up the corners of her generous mouth, softened her entire features to a near-beauty, and filled her eyes, deepening their blue.

"You'd like to see Cra . . . Mr. Roper, I suppose?" she corrected herself almost before Ellen had time to realise what she said. "I don't think he's gone yet. Someone said he'd gone to the doctors' common room with a colleague. I'll go and see."

She was gone, taking with her, Ellen felt, puzzled, a sensation of dependability, of someone to whom she could turn in this her moment of self-bewilderment and self-distrust. The nurse who had first spoken to her came along and said she was to be taken to X-Ray, and, turning her head slightly as though in mute acknowledgement, she felt herself wheeled away.

In the doctors' common room Craig was, for the first time, giving vent to the feelings which had begun to worry him where Grey Walls was concerned. The whole thing had started because Bob Anderson had casually issued an invitation from his wife and himself for Craig to spend his Christmas leave with them.

"I know you're scheduled to be Father Christmas on the kiddies' ward," Bob had said, "and that you're carving the turkey—all of 'em—in the main dining-hall at dinner time, and for all I know Home Sister's roped you in to carve the nurses' turkeys as well! You deserve some time off, some time for you to enjoy your own Christmas . . . try it in the middle of family festivities! At least I think I can promise you won't be bored!"

"I'm never bored," Craig protested as he had always protested, then he stopped, because now it simply wasn't true any more. He *was* bored, he realised with a faint sense of shock. He was bored by his own company, night after night. He was sick of the sight of the television, of the silent radio, because somehow to switch either of them on and to fill the house with sound made the atmosphere more lonely than ever.

"Come and give it a try," Bob urged. "We'll love to have you, and you'll know what you'll find yourself doing next year this time, if you're lucky! This'll be the first free Christmas I've had in four years . . . free for the two-day holiday, that is. We shall be a family party Christmas Day, and have friends in on Boxing Day, but you'll know most of them, nearly all are St. Jude's people or in some way attached. Maybe it's not wise, but one tends to get a bit that way when one isn't free to move about a lot in other circles. I promise you a happy and friendly time, though!"

"Thanks." Craig knew he was sounding definitely unfriendly, but there seemed little he could do about it. He hedged carefully. "I . . . my plans aren't made yet," he said. "Can I let you know a day or so ahead?"

What would Nona be doing this Christmas holiday? he wondered. Casualty remained open all through the season, there were so many unforeseen accidents which happened to people when they were enjoying themselves and hadn't as great a thought of possible dangers as at more normal, rational times. He remembered one incident in the Emley General when a child had been badly burned when the electric lights on a tree had caused a fire. And another time, when a small girl had been too intent upon helping Mummy and cut herself badly when she had pulled over a dumb waiter full of bottles, glasses and decanters.

Would Nona be on duty, would there be—as he expected there would be—a rota which left her free part of each day, and if so, what part of Christmas Day and Boxing Day would be hers to do with as she willed?

He knew she was in the nurses' choir and that she, along with the others, would be walking the wards, singing, lanterns lit and voices atune . . . but he would have no part in that, and he could not even dare to hope she would think of him . . . how could he, when there was this other, unknown man in the flat next door to think about as well?

"You might as well see first hand how the other half live," Bob joked. "We were the rash ones! We married in my first year as a registrar, and look at us now! Four kids—but no mortgage any more—both of us a little more . . . let's say 'comfortable' in appearance, and with a few more lines on our faces, but some of them are laughter lines, remember! The point is, we were too crazy about each other to have the sense to wait, as you've done. . . ."

"Shut up, can't you!" Bob was silent immediately, but he looked at Craig with the discerning eye of a colleague and Craig knew the moment he had dreaded was upon him, the moment when he must tell the truth to Bob, to everyone and anyone who asked him, regardless of the consequences.

"There isn't going to be any Christmas like the one you describe, for me, not ever!" he said, and he could never have guessed at the desolation in his tone. "I wasn't going to say anything to anyone, at least not until after Christmas, but it isn't just the thought of spending the festive season alone in that house which is bothering me. It's the knowledge that, now I've bought it, I'm lumbered with it, just me, by myself, for ever! There isn't going to be any wedding after all, you see, Bob. I'm thinking of looking for a small flat for myself or taking a small suite in one of the commercial hotels, and putting Grey Walls up for sale, even though it's a bad time of the year to sell a house, or so I understand."

"But. . . ." Bob was bewildered. His honest brown eyes behind his spectacles gleamed their sympathy, but looking into Craig's face he felt sympathy was perhaps not what was really needed. The man looked angry and grieved. Yes, that was the word, grieved. He'd never looked like this before, although Bob's wife had told him there were rumours a-plenty flying to the effect that all was not well with the new S.S.O. and his fiancée.

"It'll blow over," Bob said uncomfortably. "She'll change her mind again, you'll see. What's really wrong? Doesn't she like Whemlybridge or has she never seen it?"

"I don't know and I don't care." Craig was almost at the end of his tether. Bob's remark that he and his wife had been too crazy about each other to have the sense to wait told him all he had never really known about his long-drawn-out engagement with Ellen. They had both been prepared to wait, and wait for a very long time. He knew now, however, that if Nona, by some miracle, told him tonight she would marry him him by special licence the moment this could be arranged, he would have leapt with joy, welcoming the idea. Even if, his thoughts ran on, it meant resigning his appointment, even if it meant starting where he would have started five years ago! He loved her so much, wanted her so badly, that nothing, he felt, would prevent him moving heaven and earth to make her his wife . . . nothing save the complication of Nona's possible refusal because of the man in the flat next door to her own.

"Sorry," he apologised gruffly as Bob continued to

stare at him. "I really don't know what I'm saying about all this. Ellen—she was my fiancée, you know—has found someone else. *That* shot me to pieces for a time, but I'd never really thought anything like that could happen to either of us. I . . . can't condemn her," he held up a restraining hand as Bob was about to say something he felt would not be very complimentary to the absent Ellen, "because I've done exactly what she did; I've found someone else as well! The trouble is," his voice fell and his hand gestured his acceptance, "I'm not certain, but I believe she is in love with someone else already."

"Why don't you ask her and find out?" The forthright Bob could see no difficulty there. "You may be imagining that bit of your troubles, anyway! I wouldn't give up that lovely house yet," he managed. "It's not easy to find exactly what suits one in a crowded town like this, not without a great deal of searching. A flat's difficult to get. I don't know what the situation's like in the commercial hotels, of course, but I do know flats are difficult *and* expensive!"

"There seem to be some small ones about," Craig ventured, but Bob shook his head.

"Not unless you know somebody who knows somebody who has a flat to let and where there's someone moving out any minute now," he said decisively. "Let me tell you about a chap I know, a young man, steady job. He works in a bank—my bank, as a matter of fact—and he and his wife had a small flat not too far away from the town centre. His wife's expecting a baby and as soon as the landlady knew about it—and it's not due for some time yet—she gave them notice to leave. 'The rule says no children,' he told me what she said to him. 'You'd better start looking for some other place at once. I have a waiting list for these flats. Single people or married couples *without* children, or without the intention of having any!' and he could do nothing about it. They had to find somewhere else. The landlady was so unpleasant about it his wife was becoming a nervous wreck!"

"And did they find somewhere?" Craig wasn't really interested, but Bob was the one real friend he had made amongst the staff, and he was quite a pleasant fellow.

"Oh, yes," Bob's grin widened. "Trust our little Staff Hoyle for *that*!" he said emphatically.

"Staff Hoyle?" Craig felt he must sound like a fool, but the mere mention of her name seemed to send the blood racing along his veins, to set his pulses hammering. With an effort he controlled himself sufficiently to say casually: "Don't tell me she's gone into estate agency business as well as leaving theatre work . . . work for which she was undoubtedly born?"

"I don't know about that," Bob said easily, "and the other was only because my banking chappie met her one night—the night of the day you had off to see about your own affairs, I believe it was—and told her the story. She said there was to be a flat close to her own vacant in next to no time, and that she'd put in a word for him with the owner. Neither he nor I know what she said, but his wife received a telephone message to say the flat was theirs and they moved in almost at once. But things like that don't happen every day, and I don't suppose there'll be another vacancy in . . . what is it? Bannister's Ryde, for some time. People in the flats there don't seem inclined to move, and I don't blame them. It might well be worth having a word with Staff Hoyle, though. At least she could ask, in readiness for if and when you *do* sell your house. I'd hang on for a bit if I were you, though. Prices may rise in the spring, and anyway, you're not at home all that much. As I've said, we'd love to have you for your Christmas break . . . and, of course, for any other off-duty you don't want to spend on your own!" he concluded a little uncomfortably, wondering just how Craig, normally so self-contained, was taking this advice.

"Thanks." Craig appeared to have accepted it all right, Bob thought. "About this man from your bank . . . how old is he? What does he look like?" He knew Bob was staring at him as though he doubted Craig's being in his right senses, but he didn't care. "Is he tall, short, fat, thin?" he shot the words at the other man.

Bob considered carefully. A precise man, he fell into a detailed explanation which finally convinced Craig there had been, after all, no grounds for all the things he had been thinking about Nona and her future.

"You say he met Staff Hoyle the night I'd been to Emley?" he persisted in his questioning, and, receiving Bob's puzzled nod of assent, he snapped his fingers.

"That explains it!" he said, laughing aloud almost in his relief. "I've been a fool," he told the astonished Bob who glanced round nervously and then relaxed as he noted they were alone in the common room and no one save himself was listening to this unexpected outburst from the S.S.O.

"I went to see Nona that night," Craig explained, so eager was he to straighten all this out in his own mind he did not realise just how much of his secret he was giving away to the understanding man beside him. "She wasn't in. Her flat-mate, Nurse somebody or other, said she'd gone to the post, been in and gone out again . . . with a friend. She didn't say anything about the 'friend' being someone who was looking for help to find a flat! I believe she did it on purpose, because I wouldn't. . . ." He broke off in mid-sentence. He'd better be fair to Avice and not make any further mistakes! Very likely she thought she was protecting Nona from the attentions of a man shortly to be married to someone else!

"She—Staff Hoyle—telephoned me, ages afterwards. I . . . it was only when she wasn't there I'd realised just why I wanted her to *be* there, why I felt I had to see her! I *did* see her. I saw her talking to a man. I saw the same man with her going into the flat next door to her own, so that seems to prove it was the one you know, and I thought it was someone she . . . she'd fallen in love with," he finished huskily.

"And you bit her head off," Bob said slowly as he knocked out his pipe into the ash-tray, "as you bit the heads off everyone you met for days afterwards. She asked to be removed from Theatre! I'm not sure," his eyes twinkled as he teased, "whether or not either of you deserve any happiness! You're both too full of your own pride." His voice dropped a tone, became a little sterner. "When I was at college," he said gravely, "I learned some lines, most of 'em I've forgotten, but a little bit sticks. It goes like this: 'Poor words unsaid, dreams that can never be, Pride holds its banner between you and me . . .' If I were you I'd go to Staff Hoyle and. . . ."

He broke off short as there was a knock on the common room door and in response to his 'Who is it?' they both sat still, listening, as the reply came clearly to them both:

"Staff Nurse Hoyle, sir. Is Mr. Roper there, please? There's someone asking for him in Casualty Theatre."

CHAPTER 15

CRAIG was at the door almost before the words had died away. His step was eager as a boy's, and his eyes alight with something neither Nona or Ellen had ever seen there, but the light, the tenderness died as soon as she spoke.

"I'm sorry to disturb you, sir," she began in a small, correct voice, "but we have a lady in Casualty who says her name is Ellen Drayton, from Emley."

Craig had often read the phrase 'time stood still', but not until this moment had he known just what the phrase might mean in actual terms of one's personal self. He pulled himself together within seconds. This was a shock for him, but how much greater the shock of Nona, if what he hoped—half-believed—was true?

"What happened?" he asked briefly, closing the door behind him, fully aware of Bob's still, listening figure in the room he had just left. "Is she . . . has she been . . . taken ill?"

"The ambulance man said she'd been knocked down, sir," Nona swallowed and made herself say the remainder of the sentence, the words which had to be said. "She'd taken a taxi to Oakfield Avenue. They think she thought the car coming along was yours . . . that it was going to stop at Grey Walls. The taxi driver said she ran in front of his vehicle, not looking to right or to left. The car was passing his and struck her."

"I see." Craig's voice was totally devoid of emotion. He could not allow himself to be emotionally involved at this point! "Is she badly hurt?" was his next question.

"I don't think so, sir," Nona held open the doors to Casualty for him, hoping there was no outward sign of the inner trembling which shook her from head to foot. "They were taking her into Casualty Theatre when I went to her. I'd just gone off duty. Apparently she was asking for me."

"I see." Craig wanted to turn to her, to put his arms about her and tell her that whatever Ellen had to say his love was hers, Nona's, and hers alone, but the Casualty nurses, two of them, *and* Casualty Sister were all watching, not openly, but . . . watching!

"In here, sir," Sister said, holding back the curtain to the cubicle at the far end of the room. Craig blessed her for her thought. Casualty Sister wasn't, by any means, the most attractive Sister at St. Jude's *or* the most popular, but she was, he felt, the most tactful. He turned to Nona as he entered the cubicle.

"Wait here, please, Staff Nurse," he said, and it was a perfect combination of order and request.

Ellen lay on the stretcher bed, her eyes looking enormous in her pale face. True to herself she did not smile in greeting, simply opened her lips and said quietly: "I didn't mean to cause a commotion, Craig. You must believe that," and equally quietly he agreed: "I do believe that. Why *did* you come?"

She had been going to tell him that she had come because she had realised she had made a mistake, that she loved him after all and that all the affair with David had been because she was tired of waiting, of being alone so much in a hospital, in a town where they had spent so much of their time together : but when she looked up into his clear, honest gaze the words would not come. She knew now what she had refused to face up to before. There had never been complete honesty between them, now there must be nothing else. They had told her she had no bones broken, that she was shocked and that she must rest for a full twenty-four hours following the bang on her head when she had been knocked to the ground. Ellen could have told them the formula, she thought vaguely. Now she knew there were no broken bones all she longed to do was to get back home to her own small room and to tell David that, if he still wanted her to go with him, to emigrate, she would go.

Not because she had suddenly found she loved him. She knew now she had never really, truly loved anyone save herself, but if David wanted her to go on her own terms—as a companion, a friend, whose friendship might one day grow to something more—then she would go.

"I came to find out what David meant when he told me there was . . . someone else for you now," she said clearly and distinctly. "He told me he'd heard . . . gossip. I wanted to see what she was like, if she . . . matched up to you!" she managed. "Won't you ask her to come here, please? I'd like to . . . see you both together."

"Nothing broken?" Craig was studying the still wet X-ray plates, and as she nodded he read the brief report. "You were lucky, Ellen," he said gravely, and she nodded again, adding on a pleading note he would never have thought to hear her use, "Please!"

He went to the curtained alcove and beckoned Nona where she stood a little apart from the others, waiting, as he had requested.

"Will you come here a moment, please, Staff Nurse?" he asked.

They stood together, looking at Ellen for a moment, and then, as though each glance was being drawn by a magnet, they looked at each other. That was what Ellen had been waiting for. She might not have known, might never know, the glory of that all-revealing love for herself, never see in a man's eyes the naked truth, the love, the longing and the near-worship she saw in Craig's eyes at that moment. She might never herself look at any man her mental and emotional self stripped bare and revealed in her clear gaze, but she could recognise that look in Nona's eyes, and know, without a word being said, that these two were meant for each other.

Moving painfully because of her bruises, she reached forward and took a hand of each of them, linking them together.

"I hope you'll both be very, very happy," she said quietly, then signalled them to go as she lay back on the pillow murmuring quietly that she would like the nurse to put her to bed for the night.

Wordlessly they stepped outside the cubicle as junior Nurse Roberts went inside. Distressed, Nona faced Craig, her cheeks flushed.

"I'm sorry, sir," she began. "I don't know what can have given your . . . friend such an idea. . . ." but Craig, unheeding the interested looks being directed at them by both staff and one or two casualty patients alike, laid his fingers on her lips.

"Don't," he said gently. And then : "Hush, my darling. It doesn't matter who or what gave her the idea so long as she has it, and so long as she isn't wrong! I've been wrong about so much, Nona, so much more than you can guess! Come into Sister's office and let me tell you about it," he suggested as that kindly, tolerant woman gestured to indicate that the office was vacant and there for his use should he require it.

Nona followed him into the small room and stood by the desk as he closed the door, leaning against it and facing her, almost compelling her to meet his gaze with his own.

"I've been proud, Nona," he said gravely, "too proud to come to you and ask for the truth. Instead I believed not what I wanted to believe, but what things seemed to be. I thought you had found another friend, a man friend. I thought that's where you were, the night I came to the flat after being to see Ellen. I saw you with a man, outside the flat. I saw the same man again, much later, and you were with him, *in* the flat next door to your own. I drew my own conclusions, and took out on everyone else what I thought was the right conclusion, no matter how unacceptable it must be!"

"I . . . he wasn't anything to do with me," Nona broke in, quite bewildered, but he smiled and nodded and she relaxed.

"I know . . . *now*," he said quietly. "Bob Anderson's told me all about him, and I ought to have guessed. It's so like you to forget about yourself and what other people might think of your actions and to go on doing what you can to help someone else! Why didn't you tell me, when you phoned that night?"

"Because you didn't give me the opportunity," Nona said quietly, "and because I too have some pride."

"We've both had too much pride," Craig said slowly, moving forward and taking her unresisting into his arms. "Pride's a very good thing, I suppose, in the right place and in the right way, but I seem to remember it's classed as one of the seven deadly sins."

"That won't go for my pride in you, will it?" Nona asked shyly. "Or in what you do . . . or what we do and have together?"

"That's a proper sort of pride," Craig murmured against her hair, and not being satisfied by the small sweep of hair he could see, could touch with his lips where it escaped from under her cap, he pulled gently until the shining mass swung about her face in the way he loved to see it. "We've so much to be proud of . . . together, Nona," he said. "But will you ever forgive me? I don't know what I'd do if there really was anyone else."

"There hasn't been and won't be, anyone else," she said equally gravely. "Trevor . . . what I had before wasn't real."

"Nor Ellen and I," he broke in, and she sighed.

"Poor Ellen!" she said quietly. "It must have hurt her . . . *her* pride, to say . . . what she said."

"I was brought up on the Bible," Craig said gravely, "I've told you that. Somewhere in Proverbs, I think it is, it says *'Pride goeth before destruction,'* but in my view, Ellen *saved* herself by what she's just done and said. She won't realise it yet, bless her, but I've a feeling she and her David will be happier now there's one barrier down for ever. I hope so," he said sincerely. "And I hope, wherever they go, they'll manage to be as happy as we shall be in Grey Walls . . . unless you'd like me to sell it and buy somewhere else instead, now?" he added, watching her.

"No, thank you," Nona shook her head. "It's your home—soon to be *my* home—and we'll be proud of it and in it . . . together!"

Casualty Sister, requiring the use of her office, peeped through the side window. What she saw made her turn instead to the second, seldom used smaller office only pressed into service in times of real emergency.

"Bring the record cards here, Nurse," she ordered. "The S.S.O. is busy, and," her eyes twinkled a little, "I don't think he's ready to be disturbed . . . not yet awhile!"